THE IMMORTAL
E. G. CREEL

This is a work of fiction. Names, characters, places, and incidents either are the product of the author's imagination or are used fictitiously. Any resemblance to actual persons, living or dead, events, or locales is entirely coincidental.

Copyright © 2021 by Eva Creel

All rights reserved. No part of this book may be reproduced or used in any manner without written permission of the copyright owner except for the use of quotations in book review.

First hardback edition December 1, 2021

Hardback cover design by LA Morris

Paperback cover design OliviaProDesign

Interior book design by Kelly Carter

ISBN 979-8-9850408-0-7 (hardback)

ISBN 979-8-9850408-2-1 (paperback)

ISBN 979-8-9850408-1-4 (ebook)

For my hubby.

Thank you for always asking if I had any dreams.

CONTENTS

Kullingrinn *(The Culling)* 1

Nykur *(Water Horse)* 22

Sigurðr ormr í auga *(Sigurd Snake in the Eye)* 27

Bjǫrn Járnsíða *(Bjorn Ironside)* 35

Ívan hinn Hræðilegi *(Ivan the Terrible)* 42

Ragnarr Loðbrók *(Ragnar Lodbrok)* 54

Þing *(Thing)* 71

The Decision 85

Ásatrúarfélagið *(High Priest)* 92

Home Is Where the Heart Is 100

Heraðvatn *(Harray Loch)* 109

Thorn of Betrayal 116

A New Island 123

Death in the Family 130

KULLINGRINN
¤ *The Culling* ¤

Was that blood on the door, or was it just my imagination? I didn't get a good look as I rushed down the hallway.

It was probably just ketchup or something from the kitchen. That made more sense. This was a luxury resort on an island paradise, so of course, it wasn't blood. Here I was, spoiling my last perfect day of vacation, thinking morbid thoughts, instead of enjoying a glass of champagne and fireworks at the farewell ceremony in the courtyard.

But what if it was blood? Someone could be hurt. I stopped at the end of the resort's hallway. One more step, and I'd be outside in the courtyard with all the other guests. I was late, and the final champagne toast had already begun. The guests were facing the courtyard stage, cheering and laughing at some joke I'd missed. One more step through the opened glass doors, and I'd be able to listen to the next punchline. Maybe I could even budge my way upfront to get a better view of the fireworks show when it started.

I was celebrating one of the, no, *the* best week of my life. All I had to do was take one more step, but as I stood looking out at the guests in the courtyard, I knew I had to go back to see if it really was blood or not.

"All right, feet, let's make this fast," I said, frustrated at myself for not being able to let it go. I turned my back to the festivities and speed-walked down the hallway. My sandals made sharp *snap* noises on the hardwood floor as I swung my arms and half-ran, half-walked back to the door.

I reminded myself, *If you think you should do something, you'd better do it. Even if it seems silly, or you'll be kicking yourself later for not trusting your intuition. Remember the time you got a horrible sunburn when falling asleep in the park. You thought you should set your phone alarm just in case you fell asleep. But did you? When you woke up, the damage was already done, and you had raccoon eyes from your sunglasses for weeks. Or the time your GPS told you to take the highway because it was a few minutes faster. You had wanted to take a different route, but you followed the GPS anyway and ended up in a four-hour traffic jam.*

I could see the door up ahead and it didn't look like there was blood on it after all. I walked up to it for a closer look, just to make sure but there was nothing, not even a smudge on the door or the frame or the *staff only* sign. I reached out and touched the spot where I thought I'd seen something, it felt damp.

"Can I help you?" whispered a dark voice directly behind my ear.

The tiny hairs on the back of my neck stood up. Cautiously, I turned my head to see who it was. A white-haired man, with a dimple in his strong chin, appeared out of nowhere. He was so close to me that I could feel the heat coming from his body and smell the beer and tobacco scent that permeated from him. The man reached over my shoulder and touched the damp door.

"Did I miss a spot?"

Like a deer in a headlight, I felt my eyes go wide as my body froze. He had me cornered, and he was smiling as if he was enjoying this moment.

Punch him in the throat, was my instant knee-jerk thought. Instead, I took a breath and smiled sweetly as I reached under his muscular arm and tickled his armpit. The look of surprise on his face made me feel braver. I used that quick moment when he involuntarily flinched his arm back to sidestep out of his reach.

"Did you know that *kilikili* means armpit in Tagalog?" I told him with a nervous giggle as I continued to step back from him.

There was a loud boom signaling that the fireworks had started. It echoed through the empty hallway like an explosion on a distant battlefield.

"Are you Filipino?" he asked, as he leaned against the door and crossed his arms.

"Half," I told him. I was feeling braver now that I didn't feel cornered. "What was on the door?" Why had I asked him that? I should have been walking away toward the crowd for safety. My inner voice told me I shouldn't be anywhere near this man, especially alone.

"Blood," is all he said.

He never offered an explanation, and I was done asking dumb questions. My throat had gone dry, making it hard to speak. Finally, in a small voice, I said the first thing that came into my mind, "You probably should've used bleach."

While fighting with all my instincts, I turned my back to him and walked away. I knew he was staring at me, I could feel it, and then I heard him laugh. It was so unnerving that I couldn't help but walk faster up the hallway toward the noise of safety. The urge to turn around was getting harder to resist. I had to know if he was behind me, so I peeked over my shoulder. The hallway was completely empty again. *What an asshole*, I thought when I felt sure I was safe. A very scary asshole.

I made it out to the courtyard just in time to watch the firework show's grand finale. The sky lit up in a brilliant display of rapid flashes, colors, and sparkles. Booms and bursts came together and were indistinguishable from one another. The guests' backs were silhouetted, and their happy faces illuminated by the multicolored explosions.

I saw my friend Rachel and smiled. She looked like she had a little too much champagne. Rachel stood with wonderous big bright eyes and a slightly slack jaw, barely holding on to her empty champagne flute; good thing it was made from plastic. She swayed ever so gently, like she was in a dream, a beautiful dream she didn't want to end. My smile grew as I watched her for a few more moments. I felt grateful I had made a friend I could share this moment with. I looked back as the last burst of fireworks illuminated the sky. Their golden glimmers sizzled and popped, reflecting over the ocean before fading out into the night. The show had ended. I took a deep breath through my nose, smelling the gunpowder, and sighed. What a beautiful ending.

The courtyard remained strangely quiet. I expected a round of applause from the guests, but they all just stood, still like statues and staring up at the sky in silence as if they didn't realize the show was over. Confused, I looked back at Rachel, but she was lying on the ground. "Oh no, Rachel." I bent down beside her and put her head in my lap. Rachel's mouth was foaming ever so slightly, and the light was so low, I couldn't be sure, but it looked like her lips had turned blue. She wasn't breathing. I looked up to shout for help, but all around me, guests were silently collapsing. Their empty plastic champagne flutes made soft pings as they bounced and rolled away from the heaps of flesh and clothes that now filled the otherwise silent courtyard.

The only sounds now were from my panicked breathing and a single pair of footsteps casually echoing in the night. A dark figure had approached the stage. My heart was pounding, and I was starting to hyperventilate. I knew who it would be. It was the same asshole who had, just minutes ago, confronted me in the hallway. What if he could hear me breathing? Putting my hand over my mouth, I forced myself to hold my breath. Did he kill everyone? Oh God, Rachel was only nineteen! I felt hot tears filling my eyes as I watched him walk onto the stage. He was carrying a long white horn over his shoulder, and it almost glowed in the dark. The horn was white as bone, just like his hair.

As he took center stage, he stretched out his arms, and looking upward, he spoke in a deep, throaty voice, *"Kullingrinn!"* Then, he raised the horn to his mouth, inhaled a long breath, and blew.

The slow sound of the horn vibrated through me. A low, constant sound was now filling the air, mixing with my grief, absorbing into every stone in the courtyard. Anyone who would come here would feel it forever, he had marked this place with tragedy. When he finished, he lowered his horn and looked straight at me. I stood up, and I ran.

Almost immediately, I tripped over a body; I got up and tripped again. "Fuck!" Without thinking, I looked behind me. The stage was empty, and I couldn't see him. Everything began to feel like it was moving in slow motion. It felt like it took ages for my legs to remember how to stand up again. Finally, I managed to get up, and I ran as fast as I could. I made it inside through the open glass doors and began running down the hallway. My footsteps were so loud as my sandals slapped against the floor. But so far, there was only the sound of my footsteps which meant he hadn't made it to the hallway yet.

The hallway made me feel so exposed, I wanted to hide. My legs began to feel weak as I desperately reached for the door with the *staff only* sign and tried to open it, but it was locked. I looked up to see if he was in the hallway yet, but he wasn't. Then, I looked behind me afraid that he'd materialize out of nowhere like he had done earlier. How had he just appeared out of nowhere?

"What if there's a hidden door," I blurted out loud, as I turned and frantically pushed on the wall paneling across the hall, but nothing happened.

Then, a memory of me slamming into a fast-food restaurant door came flashing into my mind. *It's pull, not push.*

I began to pull on the wall paneling, I almost couldn't believe it as the door swung open. I stepped inside and swiftly closed it behind me. Should I wait for him to pass and then double back? But what if he saw the last second of the door closing behind me? I didn't want to run by the dead guests, but maybe he wouldn't expect I would. Then, where would I go? There was a village just outside of the resort, I could find help there.

Lightly pressing my ear to the door, I listened, but I couldn't hear anything. Looking behind me, I saw a spiraling metal staircase. Maybe there was another way out, or somewhere better to hide. I put my ear back to the door. But this time I couldn't shake the feeling he was on the other side of the door, patiently waiting like a cat for his mouse to come out of her hiding place.

He knew about this door. What if it was a dead-end? I had already given away any advantage of a lead, and I was too afraid to go back out of the way I had come in. I backed up slowly and tiptoed up the staircase, watching over my shoulder until the door was no longer in view and hoping that there was another way out.

At the top of the stairs, I found myself in a cozy little room filled with bookshelves. Along the back wall was an antique desk, and on the desk sat a *laptop!* I hurried to the computer and opened the lid. Maybe the internet was fixed, it had been down all day, but if I could get it to work, I could call for help.

Damn, it was password protected. *Maybe it's something easy*, I thought, *like 'password.'* No luck, but it was worth a shot. I started to look around the desk, as it might be written down. Moving around some unopened envelopes, I found a letter opener but no password. The letter opener was like a thin dagger with a sharp double-bladed edge. Its brass handle was a double-tailed mermaid, her tails twisting around each other and onto the blade itself.

That's when I heard someone clear their throat. Instinctively, I grabbed the letter opener and looked up, fiercely pointing in the direction of—

"Mr. Lodbrok?" In my rush for the laptop, I hadn't noticed old Mr. Lodbrok, the resort owner, sitting in a leather armchair in the corner. He had a small rectangular table next to him with a stained-glass lamp sitting upon it.

Reaching down into his lap, Mr. Lodbrok picked up his dinner plate. His napkin and silverware lying neatly on top of it, he sat the plate down on the table beside him. Slowly, he grabbed his walking cane which was propped up next to him and lifted it toward me in a gesture of self-defense.

"*En-garde*, Ms. Anderson!" He chuckled, putting down his cane as I lowered what I realized was his letter opener. "The password is *lykilorð*," he said with a mischievous smile through his white beard. I picked up the laptop and tried to repeat the word.

"Lickeeloth? Can you spell that?" I asked him.

"Bring it to me so I can type it in for you. It means, *password*, in a language as old as I am."

How clever, I thought, and I couldn't help but smile for a moment as I handed Mr. Lodbrok the laptop.

"Something happened in the courtyard. We need to call for help," I told him, as calmly as I could while he began to type in the letters with one finger. I was getting anxious again, I didn't want to scare poor Mr. Lodbrok with the details, but I needed to get into his computer. Right now, it was our only lifeline. Or was it?

"Do you have a phone in your office?" I asked, but he didn't answer. He was concentrating on typing in his password. He was so slow, and I was getting impatient. I had to remind myself it wasn't his fault. Hadn't he told me earlier this week that he was celebrating his 100th birthday soon? The fact that he even knew how to use a laptop was impressive.

As I waited, I looked closely at his face. Maybe he was joking about his age. Mr. Lodbrok would say the craziest things to the guests when he mingled with them during mealtimes. He looked like he might be in his eighties as he sat in his chair in front of me. He looked younger somehow from when I saw him last.

"Mr. Lodbrok, this light is very flattering on you. I swear you look twenty years younger."

He laughed, "Only twenty years? How disappointing. Here, Ms. Anderson, I'm sorry, but I think the Wi-Fi is still not working, and unfortunately, I don't have a phone, but my brother does."

His brother? I thought, as I clicked on the internet icon. Damn, he was right. Maybe there was a router around here somewhere. I started to look along the wall, and that's when I saw a glass of champagne sitting behind the stained-glass lamp.

"Don't drink the champagne!" I swept my hand impulsively across the table, knocking over his lamp, spilling the glass, which was in a crystal champagne flute not a plastic one, and sending his dinner plate, napkin, and silverware crashing to the floor.

"Ms. Anderson," said Mr. Lodbrok, as he tapped disapproving fingers on his armchair, "what are we going to do with you?" I looked at the mess I made and leaned down to pick up the lamp. Luckily, it didn't look broken. Then, my stomach dropped, and I stopped and stared. On the floor, previously hidden by his napkin, was Mr. Lodbrok's half-eaten dinner. A bloody, red, raw human heart.

I felt sick and betrayed; worst of all, I felt so stupid as I realized who Mr. Lodbrok's brother was. Slowly, I got up, leaving his laptop on the floor, but I held on tight to his double-bladed, mermaid letter opener. I looked him straight in the eyes and asked, "What does k-kullin-grinn mean?" My voice was only a whisper as I sounded out what I had heard his brother say in the courtyard.

"It means the culling," Mr. Lodbrok replied with hungry eyes.

"I think it's time for me to leave, Mr. Lodbrok." I began to step over the mess on the floor and make my way back to the stairs.

"Is it, Ms. Anderson?" He began to stand up. I threateningly pointed his letter opener at him.

"No need to stand. I'll see myself out." Stepping carefully around the last of the chaos on the floor, I held the letter opener so tightly my knuckles turned white. I was focused entirely on Mr. Lodbrok that I wasn't paying attention to where I was backing up. My shoulder ran into the door frame behind me. My next step should take me out of the door. Instead, I bumped straight into his brother.

"Ivar, it's good of you to join us."

I roared and lashed out like a cornered animal, swinging my arm up and plunging the blade of the letter opener deep into Ivar's neck. The look of surprise on Ivar's face was pure shock. *That was for Rachel, that was for all of them, that was for me!* I was ready to watch him choke, but he did no such thing. Instead, he locked eyes with me, and his expression changed from shock to rage in less than a heartbeat. He slowly pulled out the blade, and as the tip pulled free of his skin, there wasn't even a mark left behind on his neck. Not a single drop of blood escaped his wound or was left on the letter opener he held in his fist.

"Ég fullyrði hana," said a now standing Mr. Lodbrok in a commanding voice. Ivar raised an interested eyebrow, and with half of a smile, he crossed his massive muscular arms and shrugged.

"Very well." He stepped ever so slightly to the side, giving me room to rush past him. I ran down the stairs, out of the hidden door, down the hallway, away from my thoughts of what just happened. I just ran.

¤ ¤ ¤

"Shall I bring her back to you, brother?"

"No. Let my new pet run loose in the yard for a while. Now come, Ivar, let us finish our reclamation in peace and quiet."

¤ ¤ ¤

I ran straight out of the front door of the resort and fell to my knees in a sobbing heap as my adrenaline began to give out. I felt shock threatening to settle in, but I had to make it to the village. Holding the stitch in my side, I focused on what I needed to do. I stood up and kept running.

Soon the lights of the resort had faded, and I was in darkness. I slowed my pace and began to walk. It was so dark I could barely see my hand in front of me or the sandy road I was following.

There was no moon, and the stars, even in their billions, did not provide enough light to guide me. Yet, I felt oddly safe, I couldn't see the monsters in the night, and the monsters couldn't see me. Or could they?

The memory of Ivar pulling the blade out from his neck crept into my mind. What was he? My thoughts were catching up with me. What had Mr. Lodbrok said that made Ivar let me go? Surely, he knew I'd go to the village to get help and report their mass murder. Unless he knew where I'd go, and it didn't bother him. I stopped as the realization came over me, but the truth of that moment was interrupted by the sounds of men laughing in the distance. I could see the glow of a few dozen lanterns coming up the road. The villagers were coming up to the resort. But they weren't carrying pitchforks and torches. They were laughing and swinging lanterns as if they had been invited.

The horn! Ivar had summoned them to the culling. *How many people lived in the village,* I wondered. If I had to make a guess, I'd say maybe fifty. How many dead guests were lying in the courtyard? Also, fifty, minus one.

Stepping off the road, I tried to crouch down in the undergrowth, but it wasn't tall enough. I would have to go deeper into the tangles to hide. It was so dark. I put my hands out in front of my face, just a couple more steps and I'd be able to hide until the villagers passed me, then I'd follow the road to the village. *I could steal a boat.* I didn't know how to drive a boat, but I'd find a manual. With that thought, my ankle caught on a vine, and I went crashing headfirst down a steep ravine where my less than quiet fall ended in a splash at the bottom. I sat up soaking wet, bruised and possibly bloody in a slow-moving, shallow creek of fresh water. My heart was pounding, but I didn't dare move an inch. Someone must have heard me falling into the creek.

I'm sure someone would've heard my graceless tumble into the ravine if it was just one person walking quietly up the road, but the band of villagers were so loud in their conversations, they didn't hear a thing. They just continued walking and passed me by. I was shivering but relieved as I watched the lanterns above me flicker through the thicket of vegetation.

Before standing up, I began to take inventory of my body. First, I wiggled my toes, check. Next, I flexed my ankles, and they seem okay, now to my knees, so far so good. Hands, elbows, shoulders, neck, head, still in one piece. I began to stand up. *Ouch!* I had a sharp pain in my chest. I took my fingers and gingerly pushed on my ribs. My fingers touched a tender spot, and I sucked in air through my teeth. Shit, my rib was bruised for sure, maybe even broken. Carefully, I finished standing up.

I felt the water running over my feet and decided to follow it downstream. It seemed like it would be easier than trying to climb up the ravine walls in the dark with an injury. If this stream can make it to the ocean, then I can too. I just focused on the current at the back of my ankles, counting each step I took. At step sixty-two, the water was gradually getting deeper and the current stronger. It was past my knees at step eighty, and it was becoming difficult to stand straight. Every step, the water pulled at my legs, making me wobble. The current slapped at me as I stood still as if to say, hurry up or get out of the way.

I could hear water echoing up ahead of me. It was too dark to see, but there must be a tunnel. I hoped it would be tall enough that I wouldn't have to crawl. The echoing got louder, and I knew I was close. I held my hand out and felt a metal grate covering the entrance, I pulled on the grate, but it was solid. *Shit*, I had reached a dead-end.

Stepping back onto the shore, I held onto the gate for balance. I could feel a patch of damp sandy beach underneath my sandals. Reaching out, I could feel a concrete wall next to the grated-off drainage tunnel. I was physically and emotionally exhausted. I needed to rest, just for a few minutes, so I sat down with my back against the wall and closed my eyes.

How did I get here? I felt so confused. None of this felt real. It was like something I'd read about or hear on the news, but it was never going to happen to me. I wondered what time it was. Had minutes passed, hours? Maybe I had fallen asleep, and this was just a nightmare.

¤ ¤ ¤

"Emma, you need to take some of your vacation time. It's use it or lose, hon." My boss Mrs. Aiken told me as we passed each other in the hospital hallway.

I'd been working at the hospital as an ultrasound technician for seventeen years, and I hardly ever took vacation days. I don't have kids, just my old fur babies Cleo and Petra, two rescue cats I picked up after college. I'm forty and single, well, that wasn't entirely true. I was married to my job. It's hard to get out and meet anyone when you work nights, weekends, and most major holidays. On my days off, I kept my phone close because chances were Mrs. Aiken would call me in anyway.

You know that bug that's going around? Well, LaToya's kid got sick, can you take her shift? Danny forgot his anniversary was today. Can you do a double? Emma, you don't have any little ones. Would you mind working Christmas? And that's how it went for seventeen years.

"Mrs. Aiken?" I said, as I stopped in the hallway and turned around. "How soon can I take my vacation days? Can they start tomorrow?" The look on Mrs. Aiken's face was a mixture of horror and pride. "I'll make it happen, Emma. How much time do you want to take?"

My mom had died when she was forty-two. At the time, my seventeen-year-old self thought that was old. Now that I was forty, I realized how young she had been. My mom was a single parent, and she worked every day to take care of me but here I was not taking care of myself.

"All of it," I replied to Mrs. Aiken. "Cleo! Petra! I'm home, and guess what, I did something crazy today." Petra came meowing with her tail up to greet me. Cleo had more important things to do, like take a nap on the top of *her* couch. She stretched out her front legs and showed her claws, then went back to sleep. I let out a laugh thinking about the look on my boss's face when I told her I'd take all my vacation days. I could just imagine her gossiping with Danny and LaToya.

She done lost her mind. Well, bless her heart, but you know I'll be calling her next week to come in anyway. Not this time, Mrs. Aiken, I thought, as I sat down on the couch and opened my laptop. "Not this time," I said out loud, as I entered my password. I didn't care where I went, but it had to be far away. Too far to be called back into work. But, heck, I didn't care where. This was a throw a dart moment! Was this what it felt like to have a midlife crisis? Because, damn, it felt good.

I typed in *last-minute vacation deals* and clicked the first ad that popped up. *Vacation bundles. Beaches. All-Inclusive. Pet Friendly.* I looked at Cleo, "Sorry, you two divas are staying with a sitter." I clicked on, *all-inclusive.* And there it was under *Last Minute Hot Deals! Ten days, nine nights, all-inclusive! Luxury resort! Adults only! But hurry, only one reservation left.* Make that no reservations left because I clicked the big golden button that read, Book Me Now. In less than forty-eight hours, I'd be sipping French champagne in French Polynesia. I grabbed a pillow from my couch and screamed into it.

I looked at my pillow, and it was soaking wet. I looked over at Cleo, and she started chirping like a bird. Why was it so humid in my apartment?

¤ ¤ ¤

"Who's Cleo?" asked an amused young man's voice. I opened my eyes. It was dawn, and I was lying with my head on a small patch of wet sand. There was a rain jacket covering me. I looked up into the delighted face of a male teenager, maybe fifteen. He looked so familiar, with his dimpled chin and blue eyes.

"She's my cat. I have two cats, Cleo and Petra." I told him. He seemed delighted by my answer. He helped me sit up, and I winced.

"You're hurt."

"Yes, my rib. I hurt it when I fell down the ravine." Why was I in a ravine? Then, the events of last night came back to me in a jolt.

"It was a good plan," he said consolingly, "avoiding the main road and trying to follow the water out to the beach. It was even low tide. Too bad about this metal grate, but you didn't know it would be here." Something about his smile was so cocky, just like a much younger version of—

"Ivar? Are you, his son?"

"Ms. Anderson, you lack imagination." He picked up his backpack that had been sitting next to us and pulled out the two tailed mermaid letter opener I had stabbed Ivar with last night. He proceeded to stab himself in the neck, making a funny crossed eyed face, then he pulled the blade out and handed it to me with a chuckle. He began to rummage through his backpack again.

My pulse quickened, and my eyes went wide with fear and wonder. The blade was real, I had proof of that as I held it in my hands, but there wasn't so much as a mark on his young neck. Ivar pulled out a metal thermos and gave me the top to use as a cup.

I immediately dropped it, "No, thank you!" No way was I drinking anything he was going to give me.

He picked the cup up, wiped off the grains of sand, and said very sincerely, "I am a murderer, a cheat, and immortal, but this," he shook the thermos, "is just hot cocoa."

Studying his face for any hint of deception, I realized that if he wanted me dead, he could have done it already, so I took the cup and let him fill it with hot cocoa. It felt so good in my cold, soggy hands.

"No, wait!" Ivar said with urgency. I froze instantly, the cup just barely touching my lips. "I brought marshmallows too." He grinned at the look of panic on my face. "Don't worry, silly mortal. You have been claimed, I can do you no harm. Drink your cup, you'll need the energy."

Claimed? An image of Thanksgiving came to my head. "So, I'm the pardoned turkey?" Ivar laughed so hard I thought the whole island would hear it.

"Yes, Ms. Anderson. I suppose you are. Now, can you stand?" Ivar pointed over his shoulder. *Damn it to hell.* There were cement stairs next to the metal drainage grate leading out of the ravine this entire time. There was even a safety rail.

At the top of the stairs, I was a little relieved to see an electric golf cart parked to transport us back to the resort. Walking up the stairs made me realize how exhausted I was. "So, now what?" I asked, as I sat down in the cart.

"Now, Ms. Anderson," Ivar took a wooden smoking pipe out of the glove box and packed it with marijuana, "you will get formally introduced to Mr. Lodbrok. Famously known as Bjorn Ironside, my king, my brother," he paused to light his pipe and take a puff, "and your master." Ivar hit the gas pedal as he exhaled, and the little cart's wheels spun in the sand until we jerked forward back on the road to the resort.

The smell from his pipe reminded me of Rachel.

¤ ¤ ¤

I was at the airport, waiting for my final flight to board. Looking around, I hoped to make eye contact with some of the passengers. This was an exciting moment for me, but they all seemed to be traveling with someone or looking down at their phones.

As I boarded the flight, a young woman with a ponytail, wearing flip flop earrings and sunglasses on her head, was behind me. While I was walking down the narrow aisle to find my seat, I noticed she smelled ever so faintly of tangerines and marijuana. She ended up having the aisle seat next to me.

"Hi! I'm Rachel," she introduced herself. "Flying makes me a little nervous."

"Me too," I told her, my foot was already beginning to tap from nerves.

"Do you want a CBD gummy? They help with anxiety." She offered me one, and it tasted like green apple. We ended up talking the entire flight. Even though she was much younger than me, I felt like I had made a new friend. Rachel had just graduated high school. Her aunt and uncle had booked the same trip I had but months ago. Then, her uncle had a stroke, so they had his ticket refunded, but her aunt gifted her ticket to Rachel as a graduation present.

"Life's short." Rachels aunt had told her. "Don't wait until you're old to start living. You might miss your chance."

¤ ¤ ¤

A lump formed in my throat when I thought about Rachel, but I couldn't let myself think about her right now because the golf cart had just stopped by the front doors of the resort. And there he was, waiting for us. Mr. Lodbrok, Bjorn Ironside, an immortal king and Ivar's brother. *My master.* Yeah, right, we'll see about that.

I nervously began to scratch one of the hundred new bug bites I got from last night's failed escape attempt. I didn't want to admit it, but when I looked at the much younger Mr. Lodbrok, he was rather handsome, which made me even more nervous. I could see the resemblance from his older self; his hair was now blond like Ivar. He was not particularly tall, but he had an athletic build. He had shaved off his beard, and I could see his chin was the same as his brother's. His eyes were greyer than blue, and he had high cheekbones. Hints of Celtic tattoos peaked out from his shirt sleeves. If I had to guess his age, I'd say he was in his late forties, maybe early fifties, which surprised me. After looking at Ivar's transformation, I thought he would be much younger, just like the young men who were now coming out of the front entrance and lining up beside him.

"Ms. Anderson?" Mr. Lodbrok extended his hand to help me out of the golf cart. "I'd like to introduce you to my men, my friends, my family." I gave him my hand, and he tucked it in his elbow as he walked me down the row of his men to introduce me to them. They all stood tall and at attention like they were soldiers. They looked so disciplined and loyal as we walked by. I couldn't help but be impressed.

"You are still their king, after all this time?" I wondered aloud. I wasn't even sure how long that meant, but it seemed extraordinary to me, if this was all true.

He nodded, "I'm their first among equals. We all walk different paths, but every hundred years, they cross for a reunion. My men know you are protected under my thralldom. Any harm to you would be a direct attack upon me. Likewise, any harm you do will seem like I inflicted it." He turned to look me square in the eyes, "So, do try to behave, Ms. Anderson, or I will revoke my protection."

An image of fifty angry immortal Vikings chasing me to the ends of the earth popped into my mind.

"I will grow old with you. I'll show you the world." Mr. Lodbrok tried to reassure me.

"And when I die, you'll eat my heart." I didn't mean to say my thoughts aloud.

Ivar chimed in, "Your driver's license says you're an organ donor, and we are a heart short. Bjorn and I had to share. Look how old he still is!" Many of the Vikings burst out laughing. "You can't show up looking like that to Viking Palooza," Ivar continued, loving the attention his comment had gotten from the men.

"No, I don't think I can, but neither can you, my very young brother. The party is for eighteen and over only," Mr. Lodbrok jested back, but Ivar looked genuinely annoyed.

"You went through my things?" I interrupted their banter and looked at Ivar.

"We went through everyone's things. Before we packed it and them on the ferry and sent it back to Tahiti, of course, the ferry will never reach the island. It will just disappear, a mystery." Ivar blew smoke into my face, "Poof!"

My blood boiled. Ivar had been stupid to give me back the letter opener; I was ready to stab out his eyes, immortal or not I was sure it would still hurt. Bjorn's grip on my arm instantly became a vise, and the sudden rigidness jolted my rib, my heart, and my body. I gave out a cry of agony. Just like that, poof. Fifty families would always wonder what happened, never getting closure, minus one.

"I've kept a change of clothes for you." Bjorn loosened his grip but didn't let go. "Come with me, Ms. Anderson. You can get cleaned up in my private suite." He began walking me through the front doors. "Ivar will meet us in my study in one hour. The men have a party to get ready for." We walked up to the second floor of the resort. This part of the building looked older with outdated carpeting instead of hardwood floors. "I'm sure you must have many questions, and I will have many answers. But first, perhaps you'd like a shower."

My legs were shaking so badly by the time we reached his suite, I wasn't sure if I would be able to stand for a shower. Mr. Lodbrok excused himself, and I took a moment to look around. He had placed a change of clothes, my boho summer dress, clean underwear, and my grey over-the-shoulder shawl on a chair in the corner. I picked them up and walked to the bathroom. On the sink's counter were a first aid kit and my toiletry bag. I put down the letter opener and my clothes and unzipped my bag, dumping its contents into the sink. Shifting through my things, I found my toothbrush, toothpaste, hairbrush with hair elastics tied to the handle, deodorant, nail clippers, my travel tampon case, and dental floss. That was it. There was no passport, no cell phone, no cash. Someone had even removed my name tag label.

I looked up at my reflection in the mirror. "Fucking hell, Emma! You do need a shower." My face was covered in dirt and sand, and my hair was full of sticks and leaves. I began by pulling the debris from my long, brown, tangled hair. Then, I carefully got undressed and looked at my rib. It felt worse than it looked, but I was sure in a few days it would look worse.

The shower had a fold-down bench. I sat with a sense of relief and turned on the water with shaking hands. I stared as the water formed little muddy rivers which ran down my legs and into the drain. The hot water poured down on my head, and I closed my eyes turning my face into its blissful current. My head was empty of thoughts for a sweet moment, but then I began to think about Rachel.

¤ ¤ ¤

"No way! Bummer, I'm a week too early." Rachel tipped down her sunglasses and rolled her eyes as she inspected the party flier. "Viking Palooza, beer, barbarians, and bikinis!" She giggled, "Not that I'm not having a great time, but this crowd is a little old, no offense, Emma. Oh gosh, I must sound so ungrateful. Can you imagine, though? My mom would totally flip out." Rachel stopped talking for a second only to kiss the picture of the Viking model on the flier, "I would give him my number. I guess I'll get plenty of party opportunities next year when I start college." Rachel tucked the flier into her beach bag and grabbed her phone. She took a selfie of us lounging in our beach chairs with our big beach hats and cocktails. "Smile! That's a really cute one. I'm so glad I met you, Emma. Hashtag besties."

¤ ¤ ¤

In the shower, my head dropped between my knees, and I threw up. The hot chocolate was now mixed with the mud slushing down the drain. I grabbed my rib and sobbed. Then, gently rocking back and forth, I hugged myself. "Hush, shhhhhh, I'm so sorry, Rachel," I whispered, trying to comfort the dead and myself. Then, taking a deep, shaky breath through my nose, I grabbed the soap and began to wash off the physical memories of last night.

When I had finished scrubbing myself clean, and I had cried myself empty, I got out of the shower and stood for a moment, wet and naked, to look myself over again. Both of my knees were scrapped up, and I had a blister on my little toe. The bug bites had me the most annoyed. I can stand pain, but itching was torture.

While towel drying my hair, I reached and opened the first aid kit. It was rather basic, some rubber gloves, lots of gauze, different sized bandages, alcohol wipes, tape, and a spray that claimed to be antibacterial and pain relieving.

I took an alcohol wipe and dabbed it at my knees. Then, I sprayed the scrapes and taped a little sterile gauze over the abrasions. I cut a piece of tape for my toe as well, and I sprayed my bug bites. Now my skin was greasy and smelled like medicine, but it still itched like crazy.

Pulling my boho dress on over my head made me wince. My dirty clothes were on the floor, so I gathered them up. My shorts, tank top, bra, and underwear were dirty and wet, so I wrapped them in a towel and sat them by the sink. My hair was still a mess, but I managed to brush all the tangles out and put it up in a ponytail. Then, I brushed my teeth and flossed. My mouth still tasted like vomit, so I brushed my teeth again.

I didn't want to leave the bathroom. It felt safe being behind a door I could lock. It made me feel like I had some control over what was happening. Looking down at my fingernails, I thought they could use a trim. As I picked up my clippers, I paused and sniffed the air. A beautiful smell was wafting through the closed bathroom door, *Coffee. Like a rat to cheese*, I thought to myself, as I packed my things back into my toiletry bag, including the letter opener, and unlocked the door.

Stepping out of the bathroom, I thought Mr. Lodbrok would

be there. Thankfully, I was still alone, but someone had visited the room. They had set up breakfast on a fold-out table by an opened window which let in a breeze from the ocean. I saw a pot of coffee and a plate of *firi firi*, Tahitian donuts, as well as a bottle of ice water. I sat down on a wicker chair and noticed a little note propped against a bottle of extra-strength acetaminophen. It read, *Dear Emma, meet us in my studio after breakfast. The door behind the bookshelf will lead you there. Best regards, Bjorn.*

"I guess we are on a first name basis now," I mumbled, as I popped two pain pills into my mouth and poured myself a cup of hot coffee. While eating my *firi firi*, I thought about what questions I wanted to ask Bjorn. Then I poured myself a second cup of coffee and stood up. I felt like I had filled myself with enough donuts and courage to meet Bjorn and Ivar. Bringing my cup of coffee to the bookshelf, I began to look for the hidden door. It was *push* this time, not *pull*.

NYKUR
¤ *Water Horse* ¤

The bookshelf opened directly into Mr. Lodbrok's—Bjorn's study. Both he and Ivar were already there. "Is it okay if I bring this?" I held up my cup of coffee.

"Yes, of course." Bjorn stood from his chair in the corner and gestured that I should sit in it. I closed the bookshelf behind me nervously and took my seat. Bjorn leaned back on his table, and Ivar sat on the arm of my chair and crossed his legs with a big grin on his face.

I was about to ask him to move, but he put his finger to his lips and whispered, "Shush. It's story time." Then, he looked at Bjorn, and I followed his gaze. Bjorn's eyes were closed, and he was gripping the edge of his table. He began to speak, slowly and thoughtfully.

"She sank one of our longboats, the Nykur. We still managed to drag her to shore. We cut into her with our axes. Each cut began to heal almost as soon as we made them but not so fast that we couldn't reach the beast's heart."

Bjorn was holding his hands in front of him now, staring but seeing them in a different time. "I remember holding the water horse's large beating heart in my hands. It never stopped beating. I still feel it ever so faintly beating inside me now. We tried to cut the heart with knives, but it would fuse faster than her flesh. We tried to cook it on hot coals; the wet pulsing muscle would sizzle and char, then when we took it off the fire, it would turn raw again. So, that's how we ate it. Raw. Biting off bits with our teeth and swallowing them whole. I'm never hungry. My stomach is forever full of pieces of her immortal beating heart. The beast was no longer alive, but she was also not truly dead, either. We sank her back in the lake where we had plucked her. She had lived for millions of years, and now we had doomed her to an unnatural death that might last for millions more. I often think we have doomed ourselves to the same fate."

Ivar stood up and walked to the bookshelf, continuing the story. "The water horse was my mother's idea. She was a seer and a sorceress and called to the Nykur with her magics. She knew if we ate its heart, it would give us, her sons, an advantage in battle. And it did! The men we shared it with became invincible. We had the whole world in our hands, and we took what we wanted! Until we grew tired of taking. There was a price she did not foresee. None of us could sire children. We grew old and older, but we did not die. My mother did, though, she had not eaten any of the Nykur's heart. But the night before her death, she told me to eat hers. She knew it would make me young again. And it did."

Bjorn finished by saying, "Every fifty years or so, we would fake our deaths and start a new life, often we'd come back claiming to be our sons. Here are my journals from a few of my lifetimes. Most of our stories, however, were lost to time." Bjorn placed his hand on his brother's shoulder. "It seems like forever, but it's only been twenty lifetimes."

"Only?" I asked. "And that's the plan, live twenty, forty, a hundred more?"

"It's not like we have a choice," Ivar snapped at me.

"I'm sorry," I tried to pick my following words more tactfully. "If you had a choice, would you become mortal again?"

Ivar put his hand over his chest. "Yes, in a heartbeat."

I began to think aloud, "If the heart is what is giving you your abilities, in theory, could simply removing it take them away?" I felt dumb asking them. They would've already thought of that. I looked down at my hands to avoid looking directly at them, but I could see Bjorn and Ivar looked at each other from the corner of my eye. They didn't say anything, so somewhat awkwardly, I continued, "Bjorn said he could still feel it beating inside him. Right?"

Bjorn leaned forward, holding his stomach, but Ivar answered, "I don't feel anything. My brother was speaking in metaphors."

Bjorn interrupted him, "No, I do feel it, brother. I thought you did too." The realization made them both momentarily speechless. "How would I get it out?" Ivar pushed on his stomach, "I mean, in theory. We heal incredibly fast, even faster than the water horse. Axes can't cut us apart as they did her. When we cut into our flesh, it's like trying to cut sand."

"Maybe try the same way it got in," I suggested. "Through your esophagus. Have you tried to induce vomiting?"

Bjorn and Ivar both let out a belly laugh. "We could drink Thor himself under the table, Emma. We never feel the need to purge," Bjorn said almost proudly.

"Endoscopic foreign body removal," I said to myself. They both looked at me like I was speaking an alien language. "It sounds complicated, but basically, you get a tube put down your throat so a tiny claw can fish out what's in your stomach. There's even a tiny camera with a light attached so you can see what you are doing. Doctors use it to remove things from their patients' stomachs that never should have been swallowed in the first place." I paused and looked at them. "Or you could just shove a fist down your throats and pull it out." Ivar laughed. I took another sip of coffee and shrugged, "Have you tried that?"

They looked at each other as if I had challenged them on the spot. Ivar took a step toward Bjorn, but I wasn't sure I wanted to witness what I thought they were about to try, so I offered a little bit of advice.

"But first, you should get an ultrasound of your stomach to

see if anything is still in there."

"Are you a healer?" Bjorn asked.

"A doctor? Oh, no, but I am a sonographer. I work the machine that takes the ultrasound, but I'm not allowed to make a diagnosis."

"Do you have any other questions for us?" Bjorn looked relatively uninterested in what I did for a living as he looked at his watch.

"Sure, okay. How old were you? When you became immortal?"

"It was late spring; Ivar had just turned twelve. I turned twenty that winter." I waited to see if he would elaborate, but that's all he would say. I looked at Ivar. *Wow, twelve,* I thought. Bjorn stood and started to collect some papers from his desk.

"How old are you now?" I asked him.

"One thousand two hundred and sixty, give or take a few years," Bjorn said. The mood had definitely changed in the room. I felt like my time for questions was running out.

"And Bjorn looks older because he didn't eat enough of..." I couldn't say human heart out loud, and thankfully I didn't have to.

Bjorn interrupted me with a short, cutting, "Yes."

I turned toward Ivar; this might be the last question they let me ask. "Whose blood was on the door?"

I expected another quick answer, but Ivar took a deep breath and, as if confessing, ended up telling me more than I wanted to know.

"I think his name was Mac or Mike. He was a computer repairman on vacation with his wife. When the internet went out, he volunteered to fix it. I didn't need help because I knew exactly why it wasn't working. I was the one who unplugged the router. On the other hand, maybe he was trying to get a break from his wife. He kept telling me it was their 25th wedding anniversary. I tried to tell him to enjoy his last day, hinted life's short, but he went looking for the router on his own. He caught me lacing the drinking glasses for the final toast. The man had more fight in him than I thought he would. Things got messier than they should have. I found his wife after. She was holding two glasses and watching the fireworks. I put my hand on her shoulder; she didn't turn around. She just said, *I knew you'd find me*, and leaned back against me. Then, she said, *I love you*, and took a sip of champagne." Ivar turned and walked abruptly out of the room.

"So, it was his heart you were eating," I said to Bjorn, as I wiped away the tears that began to overflow onto my cheek.

"Do you eat meat, Emma? It's convenient for you in this time, all wrapped up in plastic in a grocery store. You don't have to hunt it or clean it. You don't have to raise it knowing it's for slaughter. It's just that, *it*, not a *he* or *she*. We all end up justifying our actions in the end. We must forgive ourselves if we are to live with ourselves."

Bjorn handed me a journal from his shelf before he opened it. "This one you may find interesting. Please feel free to look around. Nothing is a secret from you anymore. I have many things to attend to, so I must leave you alone. Emma, the new guests have already begun to arrive for Viking Palooza. For their sake, please stay out of sight." He walked through his hidden door and closed the bookshelf behind him.

SIGURÐR ORMR Í AUGA
¤ *Sigurd Snake in the Eye* ¤

I opened the journal Bjorn gave me, on the first page was a drawing of the two-tailed mermaid just like the letter opener that was currently lying between my toothbrush and deodorant. A small inscription on the side of the drawing read, "1812, figurehead from my ship, Akrostolio." The pages felt fragile, and Bjorn's penmanship was beautiful, but I couldn't read it very well. I think he was writing about a revolution. I flipped gently through the pages to look for more drawings. Then, I placed the journal back on its shelf.

    A square wooden box caught my eye. I opened the lid, and it was filled with old photographs. Unfortunately, the light wasn't very good in the study, so I took the box and a few more journals from the shelf in my arms as well as my empty coffee cup and brought them back through the bookshelf to Bjorn's bedroom.

    I sat on Bjorn's bed and opened the box again. The first photo was in color. A gorgeous young woman stared back at me, naked with her dark hair cascading over her breasts, laughing at the camera. On the back, written in a feminine hand, *All we need is love! -Rosaline 1967.* The following photo was in black and white. Her light hair was pinned up in a bun, and she wore a cameo around her neck. I flipped it over, *All my love, forever and a day. – Elizabeth 1910.* Next was a darker woman with curly black hair. She was wrapped in a see-through shawl, the inscription read,

Mon Coeur t'appartient. Mary 1910.

"How scandalous, Mr. Lodbrok. Two women in the same year." Next was *Jane, 1843*. She was standing outside with a frown on her face. There was no other inscription other than her first name and a date. Then, there was a golden locket wrapped in a piece of fine, fragile fabric, inside a portrait was painted of a woman with red hair, with the initials *E.C.* engraved on the back. Lastly, there was a simple piece of wood. I ran my hand over its perfectly smooth and waxed corners. I couldn't read the name; it was carved in runes, but I was sure it was the name of a woman.

I put everything back into the box the same way I had found it. The thought of having someone remember me forever was tragically romantic. I let out a sigh as I put the lid back on. I wondered if my photo would ever be added to this box. A big part of me hoped it would and then there was the little rational part of me that screamed, *Stockholm Syndrome already?*

Getting off the bed, I walked over to the exit door. There wasn't a peephole, so I pressed my ear against it and listened. I didn't hear anything. *Maybe the hallway is empty.* I unlocked the door and began to turn the knob. That's when I heard a suitcase rolling past and the faint sound of laughter. I locked the door again and pressed my back to it. Slowly, I slid to the floor, and I hugged my legs.

Freedom could be just on the other side of the door, and I would've risked it if the consequences were my own. But these guests were just kids, young adults like Rachel. Her life was only just beginning. I was a middle-aged woman who chose not to start living her life until now. These young people should not suffer because of my decisions. They are not responsible for rescuing me. If anything, I was responsible for keeping them safe.

Something else occurred to me. *Did I even want to be saved? What would that even mean, I get my old life back? How would I explain being the only survivor of a missing ferry? The police would question me, and if I told the truth, I'd probably end up in a mental institution. If I lied, I'd probably end up in prison.*

If I was being honest with myself, I didn't want to go back to the way things were. So, I got up and walked to the bed, picking up a journal. I took it to the wicker chair and tried to curl my legs up under me, but my knees hurt, so I put my feet up on the little table and began to thumb through the pages.

This journal wasn't written in English, but it didn't look as old as the first. As I was flipping through the pages, a photo fell out. It looked like a younger Bjorn and a slightly older Ivar standing by a WWI plane. On the back was written, *mit meinem Bruder, Manfred 1918*. I stared out of the window, listened to the tropical birds, and daydreamed what it must have been like to be immortal in WWI and then WWII. I wondered what side of history Bjorn and Ivar were on. A big yawn escaped my mouth, and I closed my eyes, *Just for a few minutes.*

¤ ¤ ¤

I was running from a burning grass and mud hut; the entire medieval village was on fire. I heard women screaming. A little girl with tears tracking down her soot-stained face grabbed my hand, "Momma? Momma?"

"Run!" I told her. "Run!" I held her hand and ran, but my feet were so heavy it felt like I was running through water. The heat from the fire was burning my face. Then, out of the smokey horizon, dark figures materialized and began to approach us. As they came closer, the smoke cleared, and I could see it was an entire platoon of immortal Nazi soldiers, led by a smirking Bjorn. He raised his gun and *BANG*.

¤ ¤ ¤

I woke with a jolt. The sun was shining directly on my face through the opened window. I could smell someone grilling nearby. The journal had fallen from my lap onto the floor, so I picked it up. It took only a moment to forget the dream and then my stomach growled. Whatever they were grilling on the beach, it smelled amazing. I closed the window and moved back to bed and opened the last journal. There was a drawing of an older man with dark hair, high cheekbones and a mostly grey beard wearing a fur collared coat.

That's when I heard a click and looked up. The bookshelf was opening. Out walked a young man with long, sun-bleached blond hair that he wore braided in a very Viking fashion. He was holding a pouch of aluminum foil in his hands.

"I was grilling, and I thought you might be hungry," he said, as he saw me with the journal. He laughed as he walked over to the little table by the window. A mouthwatering smell trailed behind the aluminum bundle. "I'm Sigurd, snake in the eye." He pointed a finger to his left eye. His pupil wasn't perfectly round but had a little slit in it like a snake. He also had a snake eating its tail tattooed around his arm. I don't know why, but I instantly liked him, maybe because he brought me food. "Is that one about me?" he asked and pointed at the journal I was holding.

"No, I don't think so. Who's this?" I turned the journal so he could see.

"That's my father. I hear you'll be meeting him soon. I haven't seen him in a few hundred years. We don't see eye to eye." He winked at me.

"Sigurd, will you join me for lunch? I can hardly read anything in these journals, and I—"

"I'd love to; I'll be right back!" Sigurd went out the front door this time, leaving it unlocked. I took both journals and the box and put them nicely together on the bed, then went to look at what Sigurd had brought me. I unfolded the aluminum bundle and found grilled pineapple and fish. I took a pinch of fish with my fingers. It was even better than it smelled. I could taste lime and coconut and something spicy with just the right amount of salt. Sigurd burst back through the door with a bucket full of chilled bottled beers.

"Did you cook this?" I asked him. He nodded. "It's one of the best things I've ever tasted. You're a genius." He just shrugged and opened two beers and handed me one. "So, your father?"

Sigurd took a big swig of beer and burped. "He's not the type for reunions, but it's Bjorn's responsibility to account for everyone. You know, to make sure we aren't in a lab being experimented on or something. Anyway, Bjorn says he's in Antarctica. Ivar volunteered to go with him to help look. Ivar has always been our father's favorite."

"I'm going to Antarctica?"

"You go wherever Bjorn goes." He opened another beer and looked over at the bed. "So, you found Ivar's box." He went over and opened the lid. "You wouldn't know it by looking at him, but Ivar is a sentimental fool. However, he wouldn't want you to know about this, not yet." He closed the lid and took it to the bookshelf. "I'll go put it back and see if I can find something about me; it will be more interesting."

I was surprised to learn the box belonged to Ivar. I thought everything in the office was Bjorn's. I ate my tropical meal and wondered what Antarctica would be like this time of year. I had nothing to wear. Maybe that's what Bjorn was doing now, trying to find me a winter jacket in a tropical paradise.

Damn, that fish was good. I took a bite of pineapple, and the warm juices dripped down my wrist.

The front door swung open wide. "Emma?" Ivar was carrying a bundle of different boxes and equipment in one hand. Over his shoulder, it looked like he had a portable ultrasound machine, and in his other hand, he had a plate with a sandwich on it. "Why was the door unlocked? Here, take the sandwich. It's peanut butter and jelly." He looked at my aluminum foil lunch. "Sigurd? Is he still here?" Ivar dropped the bundle next to the bed.

"He's in the study, looking for something interesting for me to read, about himself. What's all this?"

Ivar walked to the bookshelf and shouted, "Brother, come!" then he returned to the bed, took the portable ultrasound machine off his shoulders, and handed it to me. "It's good that Sigurd is here. He will want to give his opinion since he was a doctor for one of his lifetimes." Sigurd was now walking over to us.

"Yes, but I hated it. When you are a doctor, it's as though the whole world is sick, and you can do so very little about it. But that was before antibiotics." Sigurd examined the ultrasound machine. "Are you with child, Emma?" he asked me confused, as Ivar took off his shirt and laid down on the bed.

"No, I'm not," I told Sigurd, as I pulled the curtains to darken the room. "I need to wash my hands. I'll be right back."

So, they were interested in my theory after all, I thought, as I washed the sticky pineapple juice off my hands. When I turned the water off, I heard Ivar and Sigurd speaking softly in their language. I took my time drying my hands to give Ivar a chance to catch his brother up on the conversation we had earlier with Bjorn. When my name came up in their conversation, I walked out and met them in the bedroom. Sigurd had a look of skepticism on his face as he handed me the ultrasound machine.

"When was the last time you ate?" I asked Ivar, as I powered the machine on.

"Last night." The realization of what I had asked came over me. What if I did find a piece of heart in Ivar's stomach, *human* heart? I took the ultrasound wand and began at his chest. "Here's your heart, see?" I pointed at the screen. "Okay, take a deep breath and hold it for me." Ivar inhaled, and I lowered the wand to his stomach. There was definitely something there. I took a photo with the machine, then I made a few measurements and took another picture. "Okay, you can relax."

It happened to me so many times before at work. The patient would ask me if everything was okay. It was never my job to tell the bad news, I would smile and say the doctor will be with you shortly. There was no doctor this time, and I wasn't sure if the information I was about to give was bad or good. I smiled and looked at Ivar and Sigurd. "Well, there's something there." I showed them the screen with the images I had taken. "You can see here is a mass; it's 45mm by 49mm, about the size of a lop-sided golf ball."

Ivar sat up and grabbed a bag he had by the bed and shoved it into Sigurd's chest. "Get it out of me, brother." Sigurd dumped out the contents of the bag onto the bed.

"Does it come with a manual?" He held up a game-console-looking device with a long wire coming out of it. "I haven't been a doctor for a very long time, Ivar. I used to bleed people to get rid of headaches, and we didn't even wash our hands back then." Sigurd was getting frustrated.

"Emma, will you try? You can't hurt me," Ivar asked, as he reached out and held my hand.

"Alright, lay down on your left side. You are going to have to swallow this tube. Do you think you can do that?" Ivar took the tube, lifted it, as if he were a sword swallower, and down the tube went, into Ivar's stomach. Then, he laid down on his left side on the bed and rolled his eyes impatiently. I took the video endoscope, turned it on, and inserted it down the tube. The video showed up on the little monitor showing the camera traveling down the tube and into Ivar's stomach.

"Fascinating," said Sigurd, as he watched over my shoulder.

"I see it. Hand me the other wire, please, the one with the little claw, and hold the monitor please, Sigurd." Squeezing the button on the top of the wire, I watched as a tiny metal claw came out and opened ready to grab. As I released the button, the claw retracted back into the wire. *Seems simple enough, okay here goes*, inserting it into Ivar's stomach, I watched on the monitor until it reached the mass, and I squeezed the button. "Okay, I got it. I'll pull out the camera first." Then, I pulled out the lump with a firm and fluid motion. Ivar sat up and pulled the tube out of his throat. He held out his hand, and I dropped what I had retrieved into his palm.

The piece of flesh was smooth and glossy. It was a dark red and seemed slightly striped as it lay in Ivar's hand. I wondered if it was human or immortal. Then, I saw it move, and so did Ivar. He stood up, and without taking his eyes off it, Ivar walked to the window and opened the curtains. He set it down on the table and got onto his knees, his hands clutched together as he watched and waited.

"It did it again! It moved; did you see that? A blade, I need a blade!" I ran to the bathroom and unzipped my toiletry bag, then ran out again and handed Ivar the letter opener. Ivar took it and sliced it across his palm, but nothing happened. So, he cut it again, more profoundly. Then, in frustration, took the letter opener and impaled his hand. He pulled the blade out, but nothing, not a single drop of blood, not even a red mark, was left behind. Ivar made a fist and began to shake. Sigurd put his hands on his brother's shoulders. "It's been in you for over a millennium. Have patience, brother. Give it a few days."

Ivar picked up his piece of immortality from the table, "Until I know more, we shouldn't speak of this to anyone."

I wondered where he was going to keep it. In a plastic bag in his pocket? Maybe they had a safe in the study. Ivar looked like he might be wondering the same thing as his eyes darted around the room. "Emma, you did well," he said, his face swimming with emotion. Then, he turned and went to the study. Sigurd picked up the medical tools and followed him, closing the bookshelf behind them. I heard arguing in their language filtering through the wall. The adrenaline of what happened was wearing off, and I began to shake. I sat down on the wicker chair by the window and drank my beer.

BJORN JÁRNSÍÐA
¤ *Bjorn Ironside* ¤

It was just after sunset when Bjorn returned. He opened the window and inhaled a deep breath of night air. The sky was an azure blue, and I could hear the faint base of party music thumping. Gently, he pulled me to the window and stood behind me. He put his chin on my shoulder as he pointed out toward the ocean. "Look just there, on the horizon," he told me, but I couldn't concentrate on the horizon. I was thinking about how our cheeks were almost touching and how he smelled like mint and coffee.

Clearing my throat, I forced myself to concentrate and looked out to where Bjorn was pointing. I could just barely make out a black spot on the water. "That's the *Bryony*, and she's a fine ship, a polar icebreaker. Her captain is an Egyptian man. I've known his family for generations. They are suspicious of me but too polite or too afraid to say anything." Bjorn moved to stand by my side as the ship's lights turned on. The *Bryony* was much easier to see now, her reflection flickered on the water in a long straight streak, like an arrow.

"I met your brother Sigurd, and he said we are going to Antarctica to look for your father."

Bjorn smiled at me, "I have a pretty good idea of where he is, since I'm the one who dropped him off. Some of *Bryony*'s crew will be taking leave here. I told them I'd bring a new cook aboard.

You can cook, right, Emma?"

"Sure, but I've never cooked for an entire crew before." Bjorn didn't seem to be worried. "I hope they have a microwave," I mumbled mostly to myself. Bjorn laughed, he thought I was joking.

"Come now Emma, grab your things, it's nearly time to go."

My shoes were still wet when I put them on, and I quickly went into the bathroom to grab my toiletry bag. "I feel a little underdressed for Antarctica." I told Bjorn, as I walked back out, then reaching for my shawl, I casually wrapped it around me. "There, that's better."

Bjorn let out another laugh and put his hands on my cheeks. His body was very nearly touching mine. "Don't worry, Emma. I'll keep you warm." Good God, he was handsome, I mean for a thousand-year-old murderous Viking. I felt my cheeks flush and only hoped my tan was dark enough to cover their betrayal.

"Ahem," Ivar's head had popped up outside the two-story window, "You ready to go, brother? Come on, Emma, I'll walk you down the ladder."

Bjorn turned off the lights in the room. It looked like we were making a window exit in the dark. I wasn't terrified of heights, but when I looked over the windows ledge, I froze. "Isn't this a bit much? I know you don't want the guests to see me, but can't I put some sunglasses on as a disguise or something?"

"I don't have any sunglasses. The longer you think about it, the worse it will seem. Just think you have already done it; you are already on the ground." Bjorn lifted me onto the window facing him, "Look at me, Emma, that's right." I felt Ivar grab my ankle. "Let Ivar show your foot where to go. Bend your knees."

Ivar placed my foot on the first rail and then he guided my other foot to the next rail. Bjorn let go of my hands one at a time, and I kept thinking, *I'm already on the ground.* Ivar said to step, and I stepped. It was only eight steps when Ivar said, "Last step," and then my foot touched the ground. Looking up, I felt much braver than when I was looking down.

Ivar began collapsing the ladder. I looked up at the open window and asked, "Is Bjorn taking the long way down?" Before Ivar even had time to answer, Bjorn jumped from the window. I let out an audible gasp and covered my mouth. He landed with a hard thump and casually stood up as if it was a normal everyday event to jump out of a two-story window.

"You almost forgot this," Bjorn handed me my toiletry bag and put his arm around my shoulders. It was much darker now, only a sliver of a moon illuminated the beach. I tried to look unimpressed at Bjorn's stunt.

"So, who's going to close the window?" I asked.

"That's Sigurd's room now," Bjorn told me, as if to say it's not his problem anymore. I felt embarrassed for leaving my dirty clothes rolled up in a towel in the bathroom.

On the shore was a rowboat with a few crates loaded into it. I got in, and before I even had a chance to sit down, Bjorn and Ivar began pushing the boat into the water. Half falling into my seat as the boat launched, I watched Ivar jump in, followed quickly by Bjorn. Both of their shoes and pants wet from the salty ocean. The boat wobbled as Bjorn grabbed the oars and sat down. Then, he began to row us into the dark waters. None of us spoke. It was like the night had cast a spell of silence. There was only the sound of the oars splashing rhythmically against the water as Bjorn rowed. Ivar stared straight ahead to the ship, but I found it hard to take my eyes off the island.

My flight should be leaving right about now. The thought made me sick to my stomach. "Thank you," I whispered, not to anyone. Maybe to the island, maybe to the universe, but I was so very grateful not to be on that flight. At this moment, I felt free. Bjorn skipped a stroke and let the boat glide over the water. I looked back at him, and as our eyes met, I could see he was smiling.

We were approaching the *Bryony*. Ivar shouted a welcome, "Three to come aboard!" They threw a rope-type ladder down the side to our boat.

"Up is easier than down. Go ahead, Emma," Bjorn said, as he helped me stand and walk over to the ladder. He was right, and I was up and into the ship with minimal effort.

The captain greeted me first and then a very excited and slightly plump woman began to shake my hand energetically. Then, with a Russian accent, she said, "Are you the cook? I've already prepared all the meal plans; taco Tuesdays is crew favorite. I'm sorry to hear the airport lost your luggage, but don't worry, you can borrow anything you like of mine. Let me show you ship's galley." We took some stairs down into the ship and turned right. "My name is Svetlana. Okay, here's galley, here's meal plan, here's locker key." She kissed both my cheeks and said, "No questions? Good. I go to Viking Palooza now, okay?"

I had at least a dozen questions, but I nodded my head in agreement. Svetlana's happiness was contagious. We walked back on deck together, and she said her goodbyes to the captain and remaining crew. In total, four crew members were going to be spending some R&R on the island. They all looked just as excited as Svetlana. Ivar was adorning them with glow stick necklaces as they climbed down to the rowboat. I waved to them from the deck of the ship, but I was not sure they saw me. Then, Svetlana began singing, "Ninety-nine bottles of beer on the wall, ninety-nine bottles of beer," and her crew joined her, "take one down, pass it around, ninety-eight bottles of beer on the wall!" I could hear Svetlana laugh as the glow of their little VIP party boat made its way to the island.

"Would you like to join me for dinner?" the captain asked us. As we began to follow him to his quarters, Bjorn struck up a conversation.

"Yes, thank you. You honor us with the invitation, Captain. I'm sorry to hear about the loss of your father. My father has told me so much about him."

Captain Youssef nodded, and as we passed one of the crew, he said, "Pull the anchor, continue our heading."

The sailor jumped to action. "Aye, Captain. Pull anchor!" He shouted and hurried away to finish his order.

Bjorn and Ivar were in deep conversation with the captain about barometric pressure and latitudes while I sat quietly and enjoyed dinner. It was a simple but delicious vegetable soup and bread rolls. I buttered my roll and bit into it. It was fresh and still warm, which made me realize I would have to make bread, maybe even from scratch. I remembered when I went through a sourdough faze, but my dough somehow got fruit fly larva in it. The gloopy jar of flour and water was wiggling with tiny worms, and it smelled awful. I tossed the whole thing in the trash, and that was the end of my bread-making experimentations.

Something soft brush up against my leg under the table. "Hello?" I looked as a ginger tabby cat came running out.

"Apollo, my cat. I see he likes you. He must know you are the new cook. I expect you will see a lot of him in the kitchen." The captain laughed and wagged a finger at me. "But don't make him fat. Everyone on this ship has a job to do, including him."

"I have two cats at home, Cleo and Petra," I told the captain, but Bjorn immediately changed the topic back to wind speeds and radars. I realized I probably shouldn't have talked about my personal life.

I thought about my tenacious duo. My neighbor was taking care of them. I had given her a spare key to my apartment and a hundred dollars. I was so nervous about leaving them behind I had put sticky notes on the food and litter box. Maybe she'll adopt them… but if she doesn't? The idea of my fur babies being put back in a shelter made me begin to feel panicked.

"Excuse me, I'm sorry. Thank you for dinner, but I'd like to review the meal plan tonight." I stood up, and so did everyone at the table.

"Yes, of course, let me show you to your quarters, Mrs. Lodbrok."

I swallowed a laugh, which made me cough and stutter. "Th-

thank you, captain, please call me Emma."

"Good night, Mom," Ivar said casually. *Play the game*, I thought, but I couldn't bring myself to call Ivar my son, so I didn't say anything. I just nodded my head.

Captain Youssef excused himself from the dinner table to give me a quick tour of his ship. We went to the galley first to get the meal plan. "Breakfast starts at 0700. Here is the dining area and communal area. We have a crew game night on Saturdays if you are interested. There's a computer, and we have Netflix. The WIFI password is taped on the side of the computer. Down the hall is the engine room, and here are the latrines. And finally, your quarters. It's nice to meet you, Emma. I hope to make you feel welcome on my ship. I'll see you at breakfast, 0700." The captain repeated one last time.

Svetlana's quarters, temporarily my quarters, was a tiny space with a single narrow bed and a locker. A reading light was fixed to the wall above the bed, and there was a little round window looking out. I felt lucky to have a room with a view and my own little space. I abandoned the meal planner on the bed and went straight to the computer in the communal area.

Sitting down, I looked over my shoulder. I didn't know how much time I'd have, so I tried to hurry as I opened an internet browser and tried to log into my social media. The screen told me an invalid password had been used. *Maybe I'm typing too fast*, I tried again. Still, it said the password was invalid. *Okay, slower this time.* I typed in my password making sure every key was correct. "Damn it!" *Okay, let's try resetting the password.* I opened my email home page and typed in my password. Invalid password. I went to my online banking. Invalid password, the computer told me. *They went through my things. That means they had my cell phone, which accessed my whole life.*

"They do say never use your birthday for your pin." Bjorn was standing behind me, but I was too angry to turn around. "But I'm just as guilty as you of that." He reached over my shoulders and began to type into the search tab. "Here, you can read about me." Bjorn went to leave but turned around at the doorway. "Emma, do you get seasick? You'll want to get some rest. A storm is coming."

My shoulders began to shake, and the screen became a messy bright blur as my eyes filled with hot tears. The euphoria I had felt from earlier was gone, and it felt like reality had just punched me in the stomach. I felt sick, Bjorn didn't even seem angry because he knew he had all the control. He was my master, and at that moment, I felt sure I would never be free again while he was still alive.

ÍVAN HINN HRÆÐILEGI
¤ *Ivan the Terrible* ¤

Breakfast was going to be late. It would've been done on time if the boat stopped moving. And yes, it turns out I do get seasick. So far, I only managed to get the coffee out. The meal plan said omelets and hash browns. I was sitting on the floor still peeling potatoes when Bjorn came into the galley. He took one look at me, then vanished into the pantry. A few moments later, he came back holding several cereal boxes and a couple of cartons of shelf-stable milk.

"The menu plan says Saturdays are omelets and hash browns," I protested weakly.

"It's a take what you can get kind of day. You can use the potatoes for lunch. I'm sorry to be the bringer of bad news, but the storm will worsen, so finish what you can for the rest of the day now. The coffee's good. Keep it coming." He left the galley with the make-your-own-breakfast supplies.

Bjorn hadn't mentioned anything about last night, but why should he? I had cried myself to sleep but I didn't want him to know that. It was the shock of it all, I felt like my life had been violated, but maybe I had just overreacted. Would I have done it differently if I were in his shoes? The first thing I did when I had access to a computer was check my social media. Maybe Bjorn had been right to lock me out of my accounts. I wondered if I'd have the self-control to *not* write my neighbor and ask her to please adopt my cats. I understood now that Bjorn was trying to protect everyone. It was just harder to let go of my life than I thought it would be.

I managed to boil the potatoes, but then the water got so rough I was afraid to use the stove for anything else. I braced myself in a corner so I wouldn't slide from one side of the room to the other and mixed mayo and mustard with the potatoes. How could anyone even think about eating? I relaxed my legs and let the next wave slide me across the kitchen to the refrigerator. I held on for dear life and put the pot of potato salad inside of it. An elastic bungee cord was attached to the refrigerator shelves to keep the food from spilling out when the door was open. I was terrified, but I shifted my thoughts to something I could control, sandwiches. I put all the ingredients in a box, braced myself in the corner again, and made sandwich after sandwich until I ran out of bread.

That's how Ivar found me, braced around a box of sandwiches on the floor. "Sandwiches, great. Everyone is starving." I pointed at the fridge but was afraid to open my mouth to speak. Ivar took the hint and found the potato salad. "Emma, you pulled through! The worst of it is over. The waters will be calming down again soon. Just in time for dinner," he said, as he loaded up the food and headed out of the galley. I wasn't worried about dinner because I was pretty sure I'd be dead before then.

You are a drama princess, my mom would've said. *You're stronger than you think, my little M&M.* I pulled myself up and stumbled out of the galley determined to find something for my seasickness. I couldn't be the only one that suffered sea sickness on this ship; there must a pill or a patch or a wrist band or something that could end my suffering.

In the dining room, Ivar and the first mate were stuffing their faces with potato salad. I felt my stomach drop to a new level. "That's a terrible shade of green you've just turned." The first mate said, as he got up from the table to walk over to me. He walked with such confidence and balance I couldn't help but admire him. "Here," he took out a plastic box from his pocket and placed a little patch behind my ear. "These things are great, prescription strength." I pressed my finger against the patch, trying to make the medicine seep through my skin faster.

I looked up at the first mate. "Thank you," I risked saying and then immediately closed my mouth again and went straight to my quarters to lay down.

Like Bjorn had predicted, the storm did calm down, and thanks to the little patch behind my ear, dinner was on time. I had just finished up the last of the dishes when Bjorn and Ivar came in. "Ivar's hungry," Bjorn told me.

"No way, I'm done. Dinner was just two hours ago; how are you hungry again?" Ivar and Bjorn were staring at each other. "I haven't been this hungry since…" he trailed off and picked up a freshly washed knife, "I was mortal," Ivar finished saying, as he took the blade and sliced it across his hand.

Ivar looked like he was in shock as he looked down at his bleeding hand. The knife had drawn blood. Quickly, I grabbed his wrist and held it over the sink, but it was strange. His cut wasn't dripping anymore. While I held his hand under the faucet, the thin red line of blood washed away, leaving his skin perfect and uninjured underneath, no evidence of the cut remained.

"Ivar, that could have been a serious injury. Maybe try pricking your fingertip for future tests." I suggested, but I didn't think Ivar was listening.

Just then, Bjorn grabbed both of my arms and looked into my eyes. His eyes darting back and forth across my face, and his grip was hurting me. I tried to tell him, but as soon as I started to open my mouth, he kissed me. My legs felt like soft butter as his lips pressed against mine. All too soon, Bjorn stopped kissing and embraced me instead. As we held each other, I thought I felt him begin to weep into my shoulder. I looked up at Ivar. He was staring at his hand and laughing in a strange, manic way. It made me laugh too and then Bjorn dried his eyes on his sleeve and began to laugh as well.

"There's ice cream in the freezer," I told them. This was a moment worth celebrating.

"I have a better idea," Bjorn whispered to me. He took my hand and led me back to his quarters. After closing his door, he took off his shirt. *Wow*, I took a moment to appreciate him. It must have taken a lot of work to look so good. "So, that's why they call you Ironside," I said, trying to flirt. He laid down on the cot and propped himself up on his elbow. "Well, what are you waiting for?"

I took a step toward him.

"The ultrasound machine is in the locker, Emma."

I felt like a total idiot. "You want an ultrasound? Of course, you want an ultrasound. Yep, just a second." Bjorn laid back down and put his hands behind his head, flexing his pecks. I kneeled on the floor and leaned over him. "Okay, deep breath and hold," I instructed. "Good, again." I began taking measurements and a photo, but this was different from Ivar's ultrasound. "Turn a little to the side for me." I tried to get a better angle. "Bjorn, when was the last time you ate?" I asked him, as I took more measurements.

"Not since dinner with the captain," he told me as he tried to get a look at the ultrasound machine's screen.

"Lay down flat again." Putting down the ultrasound, I took my hands and pushed on his stomach. I could feel it, a large, hard mass at least the size of a baseball. "It's bigger than Ivar's," I told him.

"Everything I have is bigger than Ivar's," he quipped back. I thought about Ivar's cut, how it fused, and thought if Bjorn had eaten several bites of the immortal heart, it most likely also fused back together inside him. "I'm not sure I can pull it out." Bjorn's mood changed immediately, he sat up, every muscle in his neck tense. "Maybe I should get Ivar. He can help." I went to stand up, but Bjorn grabbed my wrist.

"You stay here, and I'll get him."

Moments later, Ivar was pushed by Bjorn into their room. Still holding a bowl of half-eaten ice cream, Ivar looked at me for an explanation. We tried for the next two hours to pull out the chunk of heart from Bjorn's stomach, but the equipment I had wasn't designed to pull something that big out of a patient. Bjorn even had us try a fishhook, but the mass was just too big, and the little metal claw too weak to pull it through his esophagus.

"I'm tired. You need a real doctor! They have all kinds of things, like lasers and I don't know… I can't do this anymore." My hands were shaking, and so was my voice. I didn't wait for permission, I just left. In my quarters, I didn't even bother to change out of my clothes before crawling into bed and falling asleep.

It felt like the second my head hit the pillow; my alarm was already going off. I got up and went to the female latrines to take my first shower on the ship. There were laminated directions with illustrations on the shower stall. Wet yourself, shut off the water, lather, and rinse. After taking the shortest shower of my life I went to the galley to start the coffee. I was surprised to see Bjorn was already there making a pot. He seemed to be in a better mood than when I had seen him last night.

"Did you sleep well?" he asked, as he poured me a cup of coffee. I nodded and took the cup. "I've come to help you with breakfast," he said with a charming smile, "because I'm going to need your help with something today."

Of course, you do. The way he was buttering me up, it felt like I was being called into work on my day off. Opening the meal planner, I read out loud, "Eggs and pancakes. You can start cracking the eggs, let's make them scrambled." In the pantry, I found the rest of the ingredients for pancakes. I enjoyed Bjorn's company, even if it was only because he wanted something.

"It's my responsibility, as King," Bjorn began as he cracked an egg, "to account for all my men. But, before we find my father, there's someone else. A long time ago, I imprisoned one of my men. His crimes, even by our older standards…" Bjorn faltered for the right words. "His blood lust was too strong. Not only had he come dangerously close to exposing our secret, but he is more monster than man."

"Where is he now?" I asked, as I measured out the flour. "In a cage, sank to the bottom of a harbor that doesn't exist anymore. The harbor itself sunk with the rising of the ocean waters. It's my job as his jailer to inspect his cage and make replacements as needed. If he ever got out, I'm confident he'd burn the whole world down. So, Emma, I need you to—"

"You need me to take away his immortality." I finished Bjorn's sentence for him. "Yes, we located his cage an hour ago. When the crew is eating breakfast, I will pull him up onto the deck. He may seem dead, but he will begin to reanimate quickly. Ivar and I will hold him down for you while you retrieve the piece of heart in his stomach. Then, when it's done, we will put him back in the cage and sink him again. It should be easy *if* we hurry. Pass the salt, please, dear."

I imagined a zombie-like monster with crabs in his beard biting off my fingers with his blackened teeth as I reach into his mouth to put a tube down his throat. "I'll need something to put in his mouth to keep him from biting me." Bjorn looked thoughtful and nodded. "What could possibly go wrong," I murmured, as the pancake batter whisked in the mixer.

Bjorn brought the food to the dining area and set the eggs and pancakes on warming trays. I went back to my quarters to put on warmer clothes. *It would be cold on deck*, I thought, as I opened Svetlana's locker. Thankfully, we had about the same shoe size. I put on a pair of heavy-looking rubber winter boots and zipped myself into a waterproof, insulated work jumper, then went to work.

It was dark on the deck except for a tungsten-toned spotlight that was shining directly on Bjorn. He was busy turning a crank that was bringing in a metal chain. There was a cold mist in the air, and the sun wouldn't rise for another hour. The *Bryony* swayed ominously in the waves now that she was anchored. Captain Youssef was on the deck loading a pistol. Apparently, Bjorn thought this was too important to have complete anonymity. Ivar handed me the tools I'd need for my part, then he went and helped Bjorn turn the crank that was bringing up the cage. I looked over the rail and saw the steel cage come out of the dark water. It felt like a nightmare; maybe it was. I poked my rib and flinched.

The cage was dripping with seaweed, and it was smaller than I thought it would be. The artificial lights of the *Bryony* cast a warm hazy glow over it as Bjorn jumped on the cage with a pair of bolt cutters to cut the keyless lock off the door. The prisoner laid motionless in a heap. Bjorn reached in to pull his stiff body out. I was fascinated as I watched Bjorn struggle to pull him out of the cage.

He wasn't anything like I had pictured him, "Does he have a name?" I asked.

"He's had many. You would know him best as Ivan the Terrible," Bjorn said and grunted, as he managed to pull him free.

"Or maybe you know him as Vlad the Impaler," Ivar added, as he bent down to help his brother straighten the body out. Then, he pinned down one of the prisoner's arms, and Bjorn pinned down the other.

"Come on, Emma, hurry!" Bjorn scolded me, as I was staring at the evil legend himself; he truly looked like the thing of nightmares.

His hair, thin beard, and skin were white as bone, making his naked body almost seem like it glowed. I pressed on his stomach, it felt cold as ice and tough as leather, but there wasn't a lump which was good news. Bjorn moved his knee onto the prisoner's arm and opened his mouth. A smell of perpetual rot leaked from within him, so putrid I covered my nose with my arm. His teeth were a dark yellow and I watched Bjorn stick in pieces of wood on both sides of his jaw to keep it open. Breathing through my mouth, I took the ultrasound machine and began to look for his stomach.

"It's hard to see anything. His organs are all, I don't know, glued together. Is that a bullet?" A gurgling noise came out of the prisoner's mouth, followed by an eruption of water. The prisoner took a deep raspy breath and opened his huge eyes. They were black as night. Forgetting about the ultrasound, I grabbed the tube and, in a panic, tried shoving it down his throat. "It's not going down!"

I changed my approach and began to wiggle instead of push. It was working. His swallow reflex was triggered, and the tube went down his throat. He began to thrash his body, so I sat on his chest. He violently moved his head back and forth making it impossible for me to get the camera inserted.

"Hold still!" I commanded, as I grabbed his hair with one hand and knocked the back of his head on the deck.

His eyes focused on me and narrowed. I could hear a growl coming out of his throat. With one hand, I guided the camera into his stomach. What I saw wasn't a smooth piece of glossy flesh like I'd seen with Ivar. Instead, it looked like a small piece of shriveled wood. I looked around inside of him a little more, but that's all I could see before he raised his hips and nearly bucked me off him. I doubled down my hold and inserted the gastroscope. Maybe it was the adrenaline or just plain luck, but I grabbed the wooden-looking piece on the first try. I pulled it out, let go of his head and dropped it into my hand and made a tight fist.

"Got it, I got it!" I said, as he arched his body and threw me off him.

Bjorn and Ivar began to drag him back to the cage. "The door,

Emma, the cage door, open it!" The prisoner's efforts to break free from his captures doubled when he saw they were trying to put him back in the cage. He let out a shriek of defiance, and the wooden blocks fell from his mouth. He began to shout in a language I didn't understand, but I didn't need to. His fury was clear, and I was sure I knew exactly what he was saying. I had to stand on top of the cage to open it, and just as I bent down to open the door, his legs kicked me square in the chest. All the wind was knocked out of me, and I fell backward over the side of the ship. I hit the water with my neck and back, and I instinctively inhaled what felt like burning lava as my body was engulfed in ice-cold water. I thought I heard gunshots and then I heard nothing. I saw nothing. I couldn't move. Was I floating up? I felt panicked and disorientated. I was surrounded by dark, and silence, and I knew I was dying. All I could do was wait for it to happen. Wasn't my life supposed to flash before my eyes? There was nothing but darkness and cold. Maybe I was wrong, or maybe I wasn't dying yet. Maybe I still had a choice.

I opened my eyes and stared at the darkness, but it wasn't empty anymore. Instead, it was pulling together and forming a beast with a long neck. It grew more prominent as it swam closer to me, stopping just inches away from my face. "Em-ma?" it hissed, and as it pulled back, its lips parted to show rows of horrible, fanged teeth. Then, with a lightning-fast lunge, it swallowed me whole. I screamed, but all that came out was water.

"Emma, Emma?" Water was pouring from my nose and mouth, and it was choking me. Someone began breathing air down my throat, and it tasted like coffee. More water came up from inside me, and I could finally breathe. I filled my lungs in fast greedy breaths followed immediately by a coughing fit and more desperate short breaths. I was shaking so violently I thought the ship was having an earthquake. Many of the crews' faces were staring down at me. I wanted to scream, but my throat was on fire. "M-monster," I managed to croak out. "M-m-m-m…"

I stuttered.

"She's in shock. Give her space." Captain Youssef was sitting me up. "It's okay, Emma, we got him, and we got you too," he whispered as he held me.

A dripping wet Bjorn pushed himself through the crowd and took my hand. "Open your fist, Emma." I looked at my hand, and I hadn't realized I was still clutching my fist. I relaxed my grip, and Bjorn uncurled my frozen fingers, but there was nothing there.

"She must have dropped it in the water." Ivar came into focus as he got closer and put his hand on his brother's shoulder.

Bjorn nodded and then looked at me. "We need to get you warmed up; I'll take her. Thank you, Captain. I am in your debt."

Bjorn carried me in his arms below to my quarters. He sat me down on the floor and started undressing me. First my boots, then he unzipped and peeled away the wet work jumper. Bjorn took off his wet clothes and picked me up again, and he laid me on my bed. He curled himself around me and began rubbing my arms for friction. Ivar came in shortly after with extra blankets and piled them on top of us. Bjorn's body was hot against my skin, but it didn't matter. I couldn't stop shaking. Then, Bjorn did something I would never have expected. He took a deep breath and began to sing in his ancient language. The song was slow and beautiful and somehow sad. He sang, and I finally stopped shaking as I drifted off to sleep.

¤ ¤ ¤

I was sitting in my bed. Apollo was purring on my lap, but then he jumped off and growled when I went to pet him. I followed him as he ran down the hall disappearing into the female latrine. *Did Apollo smell a mouse?* I went in after him, and he was backed in a corner, his tail thick as he hissed at me. "What kind of *devil* has gotten into you?" I asked him, but just then, I caught my reflection in the mirror. My hair and skin were bone white, and my pupils were so huge that they made my bloodshot eyes look solid black.

¤ ¤ ¤

I woke up, breathing hard. My heart was pounding as I sat up. The blankets fell to my waist, and I realized I was naked. Bjorn was asleep next to me, blocking me in against the wall. I was sweating, and my throat hurt. I felt so thirsty. I decided to scooch my way out through the foot of the bed instead of waking Bjorn. Rummaging through Svetlana's locker I picked out one of her t-shirts, it hung nicely below my butt, and I put my sandals on and went to the galley.

Apollo was there, he greeted me with his tail up and meowed. "Don't worry. I know what you want." I got myself a big glass of water and poured a little milk on a plate for Apollo. Sitting next to him on the floor, I watched as he lapped it up purring.

"There you are." Bjorn was standing in the doorway wearing nothing but a pair of boxers. He was a beautiful man, and I had a feeling he knew that all too well. "Emma, I'm so sorry," he said, as he sat on the floor with me. His beautiful face looked remorsefully down at the floor. "I said I would protect you." Bjorn wrapped an arm around my shoulder. "When I saw you go overboard, I'm so sorry, I couldn't jump in to save you right away." I was confused, was he not the one who saved me? "I had to hold on to the prisoner. I couldn't let him escape. The things he would've done, I couldn't let him go. I had to finish it. When Ivar let go of him to jump in after you, and the prisoner slipped out of my hold... Luckily, the captain was ready with his pistol and shot him in the chest and head. It disorientated him just long enough for me to shove him back in the cage, and the captain and I locked and threw the cage overboard. Then, we looked over the side and didn't see you or Ivar. I just stood there waiting, expecting both of your heads to pop up any second. The crew heard the gunshots, and they were all on the deck asking what happened.

"Finally, Ivar came up to the surface, but it was just him, he couldn't find you, and he was struggling himself. The captain threw him a life preserver, and then I jumped in. You had been under so long; I thought you were—"

I interrupted him, "Yes, I thought I was too. But here we are."

Maybe it was the icy cold water. I'd read stories about people being submerged in for over an hour and still surviving. Or maybe it just seemed like a lot longer than it was. For me, it felt like… But I couldn't finish my thought because my throat grew a lump, and I began to cry. Bjorn put his other arm around me and held me for a few moments before carrying me back to bed.

My throat burned, and my head hurt. "What time is it?" I asked Bjorn who was sitting at the edge of my bed. "Two a.m. You've slept nearly nineteen hours. Are you still tired?" Thirsty, yes. Tired? Not at all. I shook my head as Bjorn handed me a glass of water, and I took a big gulp. "Would you like to see the Southern Lights?" he asked me, as I took another big gulp and nodded. A smile began to spread across my face.

RAGNARR LOÐBRÓK
¤ *Ragnar Lodbrok* ¤

I pulled on a grey sweater over Svetlana's t-shirt. It had a small hole in the elbow, and I decided I'd fix it for her when I had time. I also borrowed a pair of stretchy thermal leggings. Svetlana had the best wool socks, they were thick and soft and purple. I pulled them on and popped my feet into her rain boots. Then, decided to head back to the galley to make some coffee.

There was a banged-up, forgotten-looking thermos in one of the cabinets. Opening it, I gave it a cautious sniff, it smelled clean. With so many men on a ship, I thought I'd better give it an extra rinse, just in case any of them thought to pee in it at any point of its history on the ship. The coffee pot sputtered and bubbled, and I couldn't help but notice how excited I was, but was it because I was going to see the Southern Lights? Or because I was going to see the Southern Lights with Bjorn?

Think of the devil, and there he was, looking very dapper in a fitted, dark grey turtleneck. "You ready to go?" he asked, as I was pouring coffee into the thermos.

"I am now," I said and tucked the thermos under my arm, leaving my other arm available for him to take if he wanted to. Apparently, he didn't because he started walking off, and I had to pick up my pace for a few steps to catch up with him.

"Let's go see the captain, I know he will want to see you, and he's on the bridge now." I hadn't been on the bridge yet. I was excited to see it and to thank the captain personally for saving my life.

"Captain?" Bjorn said, "Look who's up."

The captain faced me, and with his hands in the air, he uttered a blessing as he walked to me and put his hands on my shoulders. "I'm so pleased to see you are doing well, Emma. You are a strong woman. I am blessed to have you on my ship." His eyes swam with emotion, and I felt so very blessed to be on his ship too.

"Thank you. So much." That was all I could manage to say. I saw he had an empty coffee cup by his captain's chair. "Would you like a refill?" I gave the thermos a little shake. "Yes, please. Come, sit. Have a cup with me. Coffee always tastes better with company."

But Bjorn interrupted him, "Thank you, Captain, but with your permission, we would like to turn off the deck lights for a few minutes. Emma has never seen the Southern Lights."

"Of course, may they shine brightly for you." The captain went to his control panel and flipped a switch. Bjorn held my hand, and we walked out of the ship's bridge together.

Bjorn covered my eyes with his hands as we walked onto the deck. "Let your eyes adjust for a minute." I was trying hard not to giggle like a schoolgirl. Being out here alone with Bjorn, felt so romantic. I couldn't believe how good it felt to be alive. The cold air smelled fresh and clean, like a brand-new start. Bjorn moved his hands from my eyes and to my hips.

Gazing out into the night, I couldn't tell where the earth ended, and heaven began. Green streaks danced across the sky and reflected into the still water like giant snakes of light. I couldn't hold the giggles back any longer; this was just too incredible. The sky began to dance again, adding in pinks with the green. Watching this was the best, *the absolute best* thing I'd ever experienced. Bjorn began to kiss my neck, and I reached a new level of euphoria, one I never dared to dream I could. I lowered my shoulders and pushed my hips into him. He pressed back against my butt, and I could feel him becoming aroused. I took his hand from my waist and helped him pull down my thermals. Bjorn bent me over, and I held onto the rail of the deck as he grabbed between my legs and guided himself inside of me in one mighty thrust. He grunted and thrust again and again until he climaxed.

I was a little taken aback as I pulled my leggings back on. Bjorn wasn't a very gentle lover, and he was, well, a relatively quick lover. The whole thing, other than the location, was regrettably unremarkable. Though I hadn't had much experience with sex, I thought maybe my expectations were too high.

I turned to Bjorn and smiled. He looked content and then kissed my forehead. "Well," he yawned, "it's going to be time to start breakfast soon. How about you take a shower? I think the meal plan said oatmeal." A shower sounded like a good idea. I still had saltwater crusted in my hair, and I felt awkwardly dirty after having sex with Bjorn on the deck.

In the shower, I went over every detail. *Bjorn kissed my forehead. Wasn't that strange?* I washed my face. *Come on, Emma, you just had sex on the deck of a ship with an insanely hot man under the Southern Lights. Let's try to enjoy that memory a little more like the neck kissing*, I thought, as I washed the salt out of my hair.

In the kitchen, I pulled out the meal planner. Bjorn was right, it was oatmeal, easy enough, but for lunch, I needed to make fresh rolls and fish. So, I'd have to get the bread started, too, or it wouldn't have enough time to rise before the bake. Bjorn came in a few minutes later and wrapped his arms around me.

"You are full of surprises," he whispered in my ear. "I'm sorry I can't stay and help with breakfast, but can I take this?" He pointed to the dented thermos.

"Sure, I'll fill it up for you." I poured him the last bit of coffee and realized I hadn't saved myself any. "Thanks, Emma, you're a sweetheart," He said, and I started a new pot.

I ate with the crew members that came down for breakfast.

They were such a happy bunch. Full of gratitude for my sticky oatmeal. "I feel a little silly." I said to the first mate, "but I don't think I ever caught your name."

He held out his hand, "I'm Richard Lopez, retired U.S. Navy, but you can call me Richie. How are you feeling? Any signs of fever or difficulty breathing?"

I shook my head. "Just a sore throat," I told him between bites of oatmeal.

"Well, you're tough as nails, that's for sure. I have some throat drops I'll bring you later. And a multivitamin if you want it. The days will be getting very short, and it will be winter soon in this hemisphere. The extra vitamin D can help with your morale."

After talking with Richie, I went back to the galley to check on the roll dough and wondered if I could replicate Sigurd's fish recipe. The computer in the common area wasn't being used, and the dough needed more time, so I did a search for recipes. *Four out of five stars, coconut lime marinade. Spice up your fish or chicken.* Okay, let's try this one. I clicked on the link. *Coconut milk, lime, fish sauce, soy sauce, fresh cilantro.* I wasn't fond of cilantro, I thought it tasted like soap, and I was pretty sure all the spices on the ship were dried. But I didn't mind improvising. *Let marinate for at least one hour.* It seemed like an easy enough recipe, even for me. I should've headed back to the galley to start the marinade, but I was curious. I typed, *missing boat Tahiti*, into the search bar. There was a news video, its header read, *Passenger boat still missing, experts argue about where the search area should be.*

"Here you go, Emma," I quickly closed the browser. It was Richie with the throat drops and vitamins.

"Thanks so much." I took the drops from him and opened one. "Lemon and honey, my favorite."

When I went back to the galley, I took out several packs of frozen fish. I also looked through the spice rack and was happy to see cilantro wasn't even an option. I decided to add black pepper and chili powder to the recipe, and instead of cilantro, I tossed in some parsley, just for color. There was canned coconut milk in the panty as well as lime juice in a big green bottle. I added some sea salt and poured the mix over the frozen fish, then covered it with cellophane. After rearranging some things in the refrigerator to make room, I thought I should go back to the computer and watch a how-to video on kneading bread dough.

"Hi, Emma. Why are you looking at bread-making tutorials?" Ivar was watching over my shoulder.

"For dinner tonight, I need to make freshly baked rolls."

"No, you don't, that was last night. You slept through Monday, remember? It's Taco Tuesday. The crew's so excited."

But I made oatmeal this morning, and oatmeal is Mondays. I looked at the date on the bottom of the computer, *damn* it was Tuesday. "Oh well, today's menu is going to be take it or leave it, I guess."

Ivar took out his phone. "Don't be like that, Emma. I'll facetime Sigurd. He'll be able to help. He was a famous chef in one of his lifetimes." The phone began to ring, and Sigurd picked up. Ivar turned the phone, so we were both on the screen. "Hey, brother, how's it going? Emma has a little meal planning problem and—"

"Is that Emma?" I heard a familiar voice as the phone image bounced out of control. Then, a very sunburnt Svetlana showed with Sigurd grinning over her shoulder. "Emma! Emma! How are you! Oh, I heard what happened. I was so worried." Svetlana said, as she held the phone. I couldn't help but smile when I saw her. It felt like I was talking to an old friend even though we had just met once.

"I'm good; I'm okay. How are you?" Svetlana looked sideways at Sigurd. "I think I'm in love. A man that can cook is so sexy." She bit her lower lip and kissed Sigurd on the cheek. "I keep telling him he's too young for me, but he keeps telling me I'm not too old for him!" Svetlana shrugged, and Sigurd wrapped his arms around her. "Now, what is wrong with my meal plan?" I filled them in, and Sigurd suggested fried flatbread for fish tacos with added cumin and onion powder to the marinade.

"Sounds so yummy. The crew is going to love it," Svetlana added, as Sigurd began to kiss her.

"Thank you!" I shouted, but they didn't stop kissing. Finally, Ivar cleared his throat and ended the call.

"I'll help you fry the bread, and might I add, you are positively glowing, Emma. What's your secret?" Ivar made a vulgar attempt to hump my chair, and I smacked him on the shoulder.

"Whatever you think you know, you mind your own business. And yes, I'd like help with the fry bread, thank you."

In the galley, I found a frier, but I'd never used one before. Luckily, Ivar seemed to know what he was doing. As he poured oil into it and plugged it in, he said, "Bjorn will be leaving soon to look for our father. I'm becoming too mortal to join him. He can travel faster without me." I looked at Ivar and couldn't tell how he felt about that.

"Are you having regrets? You could always swallow your piece of heart again." I suggested.

His expression was very serious when he looked at me. "No," he said sternly.

"What did you do with it anyway? Is it in a plastic bag in your pocket?" I smiled like it was a joke, but a part of me thought that's where it was. "I put it in the safest place I could think of," he said and winked at me. "I had Sigurd swallow it." That was clever I thought. Definitely safer in Sigurd's stomach unless…

"What if the pieces fuse together? Or do you think Sigurd will want to stay immortal?"

"The other night when you gave Bjorn the ultrasound and tried to remove his piece. Well, when you left, we tried plan B, and it worked!" Ivar told me with a grin on his face.

"Plan B?" I was confused, I didn't know there was an alternative plan.

"You said it yourself, *or we could just shove a fist down each other's throats and pull it out*. It took a lot of pulling, but it worked! Then, Bjorn ate it again, of course." Ivar rolled his eyes. "He needs to stay invulnerable to find our father, and what were we going to do with it? Put it in a plastic bag and stick it in our pocket?" Ivar gave me a sideways glance, and we both started laughing.

"You know, I Googled you a little bit," I confessed, as we rolled out the dough balls.

"Don't believe everything you read. History is a bunch of bored mortals guessing what happened and trying to make things sound far more interesting than they really were, so they can call themselves experts. And I'm pretty sure one of my brothers filled out my Wikipedia page."

Ivar tested the hot oil with his finger.

"Ouch! Look at that. I'm healing a little slower every day," he said, as he looked at his burned and blistering finger.

"You are going to make me throw up, stop that!" I scolded him and thought about kicking him out of the kitchen, but I had another question. "So, Ivar *the Boneless*, what's that about?"

Ivar shook his head. "That's a perfect example of *experts* arguing about something *so obvious* but still getting it wrong." Ivar held out his hand and bent his thumb down to his wrist. "I'm double-jointed. I would play around and bend myself into shapes when I was a child. My father thought it was funny; he said it was as if I didn't have any bones and the nickname stuck." Ivar began to drop the raw dough into the frier.

"Since you plan on staying mortal, what do you want to do with your last life?" I asked and wondered myself what he would want to do that he hadn't already done. "I'll stay with Bjorn for a couple of years. I must until I can pass for eighteen. Then I'll find a woman who will have me and hopefully bear me many children." Ivar was smiling, as he plopped another dough into the frier. "I'll drive a minivan and be a stay-at-home dad. Maybe I'll become a writer and write fiction about immortal Vikings.

Hopefully, my woman can cook because I want to get fat!"

I would never have pictured Ivar as a family man. When I looked over at him, he looked happily lost in a daydream of his simple, perfect, and final future.

Frybread, fish taco Tuesday was a big hit with the crew. After dinner, they formed a line outside of the galley and began cheering. I walked out with my grease-stained apron still on, and each one of the crew shook my hand. They were starting to feel like family. It was amazing how food had that power. I looked over at Bjorn; he was smiling and clapping too. *My family*, I thought as I looked at him, and I felt so fortunate he had chosen me because, at that moment, I realized I had chosen him too.

After cleaning the galley, I went to go find Bjorn. He wasn't in his quarters, so I looked on the deck. It was already dark and so much colder than yesterday. I wouldn't be able to stay out here long without a jacket. The water was turning to ice and the ship sliced her way through, creating a slushy path behind her. Bjorn and Ivar were standing with one of the crates they had brought from the island. Ivar was smoking his pipe. The red glow partially illuminated his face every time he took a puff.

"Emma, do you like fireworks?" Bjorn asked, as he cracked open the crate with a crowbar. "These are special flares. We will fire them off every hour to signal our father, so he knows I'm looking for him. Would you like to shoot the first one?" Bjorn wrapped his arms around me and put the flare launcher in my hand, then holding my hand he pointed it up and away from the ship. "Okay, when you're ready, squeeze the trigger."

I quickly kissed him on the cheek. "For luck," I said and squeezed the trigger. The shot was so loud, I let out a shout of surprise and excitement. The flare sailed up in the air, made a pop, and began to trail like a sparkling fountain firework, crackling on its way down.

"If he sees it, he'll know to meet me where I dropped him off." As much as I wanted to stay in Bjorn's arms it was just too cold outside, so I gave him back the flare launcher and went back below deck. I made sure the coffee was fresh and hot for the night shift and then went to bed.

Wednesday's meal plan said toast and eggs with orange juice. But I'd used up all the sandwich-style bread during the storm, so I decided to use the tortilla wraps since I didn't use them for Taco Tuesday. There was concentrated orange juice in the freezer that I poured into a giant cooler with a spout so the crew could help themselves. The wind was picking up outside. Whenever a crew member came down the stairs, the galley would get a cold whoosh of fresh air. I was glad to be by the stove. The galley was the warmest room on the ship, with the exception of the engine room. So, when the captain came to see me, I first thought that he just wanted to warm up for a little bit, but he told me it was Richie's birthday and asked if I had time, if I could make him a cake. I told him it wouldn't be pretty, but it will be made with love and ready by dinner.

"Cake, cake." I was talking to myself. Why was there not an instant cake mix in the pantry? I realized I would have to make one from scratch, which I'd never done before. But lucky for me, lots of other people had, so I headed to the common room to Google it. I wondered what kind of cake Richie liked. I was a fan of lemon, and lemon cake didn't need frosting, just drizzled glaze. Typing in *easy lemon cake for beginners*, I scrolled through the recipes. They all said they were easy, but there were so many directions. I wasn't going to be able to remember them all. *Maybe there's a printer for the computer.* Baking this cake would be so much easier if I had my cell phone, I could just pull up the recipe in the galley instead of going back and forth to the computer.

I looked around the room, there was a storage closet next to the computer, so I opened it, but it was just filled with board games. I ended up using the back of a Yahtzee scoreboard and one of the little pencils the game came with to make notes. "One cup sugar, half a cup butter, two eggs," I mumbled, as I tried to write small but legible. Just then, Richie walked in. "Emma, first taco Tuesday and now breakfast burritos? You are a woman after my own heart."

The birthday boy himself. *Play it cool*, I thought. "You're welcome; really, it was no problem." *Crap*, he was walking toward me.

"Yum, lemon cake. Did someone tell you it was my birthday today?" I think I officially ruined the surprise.

"Maybe. Richie, can I borrow your phone for an hour? I *might* be making a cake, and I *might* have a better chance at making it eatable if I didn't have to write the directions down on the back of a Yahtzee score pad."

He laughed, "Sure, here you go. You don't have a phone?"

I shook my head. "It's on the bottom of the ocean," I told him truthfully.

"Well, as long as mine doesn't end up on the bottom with yours, you can borrow it. Here, I'll log you into the WIFI. When you are done making the cake, I'll be happy to come and get it back and maybe help lick the buttercream frosting spoon." Crap, he wants frosting on his cake.

"Okay, happy birthday, Richie."

I brought Richie's phone back to the galley, and occasionally, it would *bing*. Richie's friends and family were sending him birthday wishes, and I felt guilty using it. Taking away his time with them on his special day didn't seem right. So, I wrote the buttercream recipe on the back of the meal planner, and after I put the cake in the oven, I went to look for Richie to give him back his phone.

I didn't want to go outside, but I was pretty sure that's where Richie would be, so I went and put a coat on from Svetlana's locker. Then, I headed to the stairs, but as I passed the galley, I saw someone rummaging through the freezer. "Hey, what are you—oh, hi, Ivar. Looking for more ice cream?" Ivar looked at me with an almost embarrassed expression.

"No, Bjorn needs something. The cake smells great; you know

it would cool fast if you brought it outside for a minute." It felt like Ivar was trying to push me out of the galley.

"Okay? I'll do that when it's done baking." I began to walk away but turned around at the last second thinking maybe Ivar could give Richie back his phone and save me the trip. "Hey, have you seen Richie? I'm trying to give him back his—" and that's when I saw it. A little red bag in Ivar's hands. "What's that?" I hadn't seen it in the freezer earlier.

"It's for our father. You weren't supposed to see it. I'm sorry, Emma, I need to go. Bjorn is getting ready to leave the ship. I'm so sorry." Ivar told me while looking down on the floor as if he were ashamed. Hiding the bag under his coat he left the galley.

I felt the blood drain away from my face. Ivar had a human heart stowed away in the freezer. The way he said he was sorry, like the loss personally affected me… *Oh my God, what if it was Rachel's heart?* I felt the gust of frigid air as Ivar opened the door and stepped out onto the deck. A second gust quickly followed, and Richie popped his head around the corner.

"It smells good in here! Ivar said you were looking for me?" I held out his phone. "Emma, are you okay? Are you getting seasick again?" Richie asked me and looked concerned.

"No, I'm… Yes, maybe." Richie pulled out another seasickness patch and handed it to me. "Here you go, Emma. I hope you feel better. If you need anything else, let me know, okay?" Richie left, and the whoosh of ice-cold air told me he was back on deck again and I was alone.

I sat on the floor, my feet hurt, my back hurt, and worst of all, I was heartbroken. Bjorn didn't come to say goodbye before he went looking for his father, but I was relieved he didn't. I cried into my apron until the cake timer went off, saying I had to get up. I washed my face in the galley sink, took out the cake, and tested it with a toothpick. Then, I grabbed a bowl and began to make buttercream frosting and tried not to think about anything other than the cake.

I hadn't put parchment paper down on the pan bottom. The directions said to, but I thought buttering the pan would be the same thing. The cake mix boxes always said grease pan well, or was it grease and flour pan well? That should've been enough, I thought. But when I tried to turn the cake out of the pan, it didn't budge an inch. The cake was completely stuck. *Well, at least I didn't burn it. I'll just serve it like this.* Taking a spatula, I spread a slightly lumpy buttercream frosting on top of the cake. It looked pretty good for being my first cake from scratch, and it felt nice to be able to make a birthday cake for someone. It made me think about my mom; she used to make me cakes for my birthday. I was pretty sure some of them were in a pan just like this, but it didn't matter to me, I thought they were the best cakes ever.

It's too bad I don't have birthday candles or sprinkles. It looked like a cake but not a birthday cake. I wanted it to be more memorable. So many people take birthdays for granted. I know I certainly had. I tried to remember what I had done to celebrate my last birthday. It was the big four zero, and I should've gone out dancing and bought myself an expensive dinner. I should've celebrated life and honored my mother for bringing me into this world, but instead, I stayed home and watched T.V. because I had work early in the morning. I took so many birthdays for granted. Now, here I was looking at a lumpy frosted lemon cake, thinking about all the times I almost died in the last week and wondering if I'll even get another birthday. Rachel won't… I tried not to think about Rachel's parents, the thought of remembering her on her birthday without her was devastating. It should've been me, not her, and I would've traded places with her if I could. But I had to remind myself it wasn't a choice between her or me; it would have been both of us.

"The living honors the dead by living!" my mother told me, as she held my hand as tight as she could the night before she passed away in her hospital bed. "It's okay, you can cry for me.

It's good to cry sometimes, but don't forget to laugh for me too. I love you, M&M."

M&M, that's when I remembered there was candy in the pantry. I pulled out a couple of bags and wrote *Happy Birthday* in multicolored candy-coated chocolates. *Now, this was a cake worthy of celebrating a birthday*, I thought and popped a handful of left-over M&Ms in my mouth. "Thanks, Mom," I said with my mouth full and smiled.

Richie and the crew loved the cake. They scraped out every bit of it from the pan, leaving just the over-baked crusty edges where the batter ran over the side a little. I decided to let the pan soak for a few minutes as I began to scrub clean the entire galley from top to bottom. I even cleaned the oven and began rearranging the pots and pans. I wanted to clean the freezer next, but all I could do was stand and stare at it.

Exhausted, I looked at the clock as it read one a.m. I'd have to get up in four hours and start breakfast. What was I thinking? I needed to go to bed. Usually, the only time I voluntarily wanted to clean was when I was about to start my period. I'd go on a cleaning spree and then not want to move for the next three days. Which made me think about the few tampons I had in my toiletry bag. If I was about to start, I knew they wouldn't be enough.

When I was in my quarters, I looked through Svetlana's locker, but I couldn't find any feminine hygiene products. It's not like I could just stop by the local Walmart at one a.m. and pick myself up a box of pads. Having my period on a ship was going to suck, but I was too tired to care about it anymore. My tampon shortage was tomorrow's problem. I changed into a t-shirt and went to sleep.

When I got up, I went straight to the latrine to check, but I hadn't started yet. *Score*, I did find a fully stocked basket with feminine products under the sink, though. My stomach felt bloated, I knew it was just a matter of time, so I put on a light pad expecting to start soon. The day went on, and nothing, even my bloating, went away. Maybe the stress from nearly dying was just delaying it.

"Bjorn sent up a flare today, which means he's heading back to the ship. We should be picking him up soon," Richie told me over dinner. "And it's a good thing too because we have another storm coming. Here," he handed me another seasickness patch. "You're going to need it."

After thanking Richie, instead of going to my quarters, I went back to the galley. If there was a big storm coming, I was going to make all the food for tomorrow tonight. Because I knew how useless it would be making anything when the ship was sailing through twenty-foot waves. I was getting used to cooking all day. My feet and back didn't hurt anymore, and I felt less tired. Although, I was running off just four hours of sleep, I felt pretty good. As I pulled the rolls out of the oven, I felt the familiar ice-cold woosh that told me someone had just come below deck.

A moment later, Bjorn was standing in the galley shaking off his winter coat. His beard was frozen solid from the moisture of his breath. I watched it begin to melt from the warmth of the open oven, and behind him stood his father! What I could see of him, through the frozen beard and wild hair, looked nothing like his portrait. He was wearing an antique-looking leather tattered vest that looked like it might have been a jacket once. Wrapped around his feet were improvised shoes made with the same-looking leather. Maybe that's where the sleeves went. His naked arms were heavily tattooed, and he stank horribly of rotten fish and body odor as he walked past me to grab two rolls, one for each hand. He began shoving his face with the fresh hot bread.

"Rum, woman. Bring me rum!" He managed to command though his mouth was nearly completely stuffed. I just stared at Bjorn with my mouth open. No way was I was going to tell this Artic, feral, bigfoot I didn't have any rum. "Father, this is Emma. I have a bottle of rum in your quarters." His father made a grunt of approval as Bjorn led him out of the galley down the hall and behind closed doors.

Ivar came rushing into the galley shortly after. He rummaged through a drawer and pulled out a small knife. Then, he ran back out again with a grin on his face. It took me a second to realize why he needed a knife. He was going to show his father he was becoming vulnerable. It was kind of cute, a thousand-year-old son wanted to show his thousand-year-old father what he could do. Some things never change, I guess. I put the rolls back in the cooled-down oven. *It will be an exciting day tomorrow*, I thought, as I turned off the lights to the galley and called it a night.

The following morning, I found Bjorn in the galley making coffee. "Good morning, Emma, I'm starting breakfast today. My father, the legend, Ragnar Lodbrok, wants to speak with you, puny mortal," he joked, as he handed me two cups of coffee and kissed my cheek.

"Should I be worried?" I asked him, as I blew on one of the cups and took a sip.

Bjorn laughed and said, "Probably, he doesn't like to be kept waiting."

"I have bread rolls in the oven already made." I thought I'd better tell him before he tried to preheat the oven and burn them all. "I better take them out just in case you forget." But Bjorn went to the oven and opened it before I could.

"Go. You little coward," he told me, and he wasn't wrong.

The ship was already beginning to sway ominously. I thought I'd better get this over with before things got worse. I moved both mugs to one hand and knocked on Ragnar's door. "Come in, witch," Ragnar ordered from his quarters.

"And we're off to a great start," I said to myself, as I walked in to meet him.

"Good morning, Mr. Lodbrok," I said politely and wondered if I should have curtsied, but the moment had already passed. "You wanted to see me?" I tried to say in the friendliest customer service voice I could muster.

Ragnar looked wholly transformed from last night. His dark hair was pulled into a tidy man bun, and he had trimmed his greying beard. Ragnar had sharp, high cheekbones and grey eyes like Bjorn. He wore Bjorn's dark grey turtleneck and jeans; his feet were bare, and his legs were crossed. He didn't stink, either. Ragnar reached out his hands for one of the cups of coffee I was holding and grunted.

"Oh, this?" I pulled them both back. "No, they're both for me." I took a sip of one, paused for a moment, and then took a sip from the other, looking him square in the eyes as I did it. His look of confusion quickly turned into a roar of laughter.

"Come, sit, sit. I humbly apologize for my lack of manners." His eyes twinkled as he watched me sit down.

"Then, I might have a cup to spare after all. If you still want one." I reached out one of the cups, and he eagerly took it from me and took a deep breath, inhaling its aroma.

"All the smells, the sounds, the people. I'm feeling overwhelmed. I've been alone for a long time. I thought I'd be happy to be off that ice dessert, but now I feel like I'm trapped in an even smaller prison. I don't even know if it's real, or if I've finally frozen solid and this is some strange hallucination my mind has produced to keep me sane." His honesty caught me off guard, and I could relate. I, too, felt like this was a strange dream, but it just kept on going. I couldn't wake up.

"So, you were a prisoner? What was your crime?"

Ragnar leaned forward toward me and said, "Treason." Then, he sat back again and took a sip of his coffee. "Against my son, the king. I tried to create sedition. Well, that's what Bjorn says. It's all about who gets to write the history in the end."

"So, what's your side of the truth then?" I asked him, and he sat up a little taller.

"Oh, it was treason." He smiled at me almost proudly. "But I didn't invite you here to talk about my story. I want you to tell me yours, and be descriptive, tell me every detail. You never know how important the smaller things might end up being."

I was sure Bjorn and Ivar had already told him the most significant parts of recent events, but I started at what I thought was the beginning. The night of the culling.

ÞING
¤ *Thing* ¤

Ragnar looked thoughtfully at me. "If only we had a few women in our crew of immortals. They would have undoubtedly solved all our problems centuries ago." Ragnar stood up, so I stood too. He embraced me briefly with a hard pat on the back. "Come, witch," he said with a tone of endearment. We walked together down the hallway, and he began to shout, "I call a thing!"

Bjorn must have heard his father because he came out of the galley to meet us. "Yes, we will call a thing immediately. Let me introduce you to the technologies of this modern time, Father." Bjorn put his arm around Ragnar and led him back to his quarters. "This is called a cell phone." He began to explain as the door shut behind them.

What a strange man, I thought, but I wondered how I would be if I were isolated from the world for decades. "Probably a little crazy too," I said to myself. "See? You're already talking to yourself." I smiled and went back to the galley.

The storm wasn't as bad as the last one had been. Or maybe I just felt better prepared this time. With the seasickness patch firmly behind my ear, I almost began to enjoy the challenge of cooking in an ever-slanting ship. It felt like something kids would pay money to try at a county fair. Or maybe a crazy game show, *Extreme Baking Edition: Lost at Sea. I'd watch that*, I thought, as I finished up the last of the dishes. I tied myself to the sink with my apron so I wouldn't fall over as I washed the last of the dishes in the sink and called it a night. I was going to skip taking a shower. The thought of being naked and an emergency happening just seemed too likely to risk, so I washed my face and neck in the sink instead before heading to bed.

Ivar was in the corridor, and he looked awful. "I'm—I'm seasick," he said between burps. "It's amazing!" Ivar burped again.

"Don't be a hero. Go get a patch from Richie," I told him, as he stumbled along the corridor.

"No, really, I'm—" He stopped and put his head against the wall. "Okay, you're right," he said and ran to the sink in the galley. I could hear his retching, and it made me feel oddly happy for him.

I had almost forgotten there was something I wanted to ask Ivar, so I followed him back to the galley. "Did your father get his thing?"

Ivar nodded and took a drink of water with his hand, "We'll have it back at the island. Most of the others are still there anyway; it just seemed the most practical," he told me and rinsed out the sink.

"I'm confused; I thought your father wanted to find something."

Ivar wiped his mouth with his sleeve and explained. "A thing is what we call an assembly. We usually have them if someone has broken our law. My father is going to make his case that it's time we all give up our immortality." Ivar began to look green again and rushed out of the galley, I assumed to find Richie.

The ship was turning in the storm, and I was restless that night. Right when I thought I might drift off to sleep, there was a crack or a bang, and I would be wide awake again. We were going back to the island, and I had mixed feeling about it. I supposed it made sense. We had to pick up Svetlana and the rest of the crew. On the other hand, it just felt like going backward, and I didn't want to think about what happened there.

Going back to the island felt like I was visiting a graveyard. Sure, cemeteries can be very beautiful and peaceful. And full of dead people just beneath the surface. With monsters lurking in the dark that looked like humans but were something different. Something other just below *their* surface.

¤ ¤ ¤

It was dark and cold, and I knew I was underwater, but I wasn't frightened. I could breathe. I saw the light drifting down through the water in beams as a long shadow passed by overhead. I began following the shadow, but I wasn't swimming. It was more like I was being dragged with it toward the surface. But I wanted to stay in the deep, where it was safe. I struggled, but the pull was too strong. My body was being dragged onto the shore, and I realized I was in a net. Bjorn was standing over me with an ax in his hands. "No! Stop, it's me, Emma!" I tried to reason with him, but he had a murderous look in his eyes. Blood splattered on his face as he hacked into my chest. He pulled out my still-beating heart with a bloody hand and made me watch as he ate it.

¤ ¤ ¤

My screams woke me up. I was shaking and angry. How dare he, how dare he cut out my heart! And then I looked around and realized where I was. I put my hand on my chest and let reality sink back in. It was just a dream, but it seemed so real, so vivid, like a memory coming to the surface of long-forgotten childhood trauma. The dream made me feel changed like I was two Emmas now instead of one.

What if there was another life inside of me? I thought about my missed period. *What if I'm pregnant?* Bjorn said he couldn't have children, but how often had I heard that from dads in the ultrasound room as they found out their wife or girlfriend was pregnant with their twins?

I jumped out of bed and went to the female latrine. Maybe

there was a pregnancy test in the neatly stocked cabinet that seemed to have everything a woman on a ship would ever need. In the back of the cabinet was a little medical kit. Inside, I found condoms, anti-fungal creams, and a pregnancy test. *Bingo!* I sat on the toilet and peed on the strip. What did I want to happen? I was forty, and I'd be pushing it age-wise, but it could be my very last chance. I read and reread the directions and waited. Just as I thought that maybe I had a defective test, the results showed up in the little window.

Not Pregnant. I was both relieved and a little sad at the same time and then I became worried. *What's wrong with me?* Why hadn't I started my period yet? It could be a cyst or could I be starting menopause already? Maybe it was just stress. I decided I would give myself an ultrasound when we were back on the island. Carefully, I wrapped the used test in a bunch of toilet paper and threw it away. Since I was already up, I went to get an early start on making breakfast.

Ivar came into the galley after dinner. The storm had passed, and by the looks of him, so had his seasickness. "It's game night. Any chance I can raid the pantry for some snacks?" I remembered seeing a bag of corn.

"How about popcorn!" I suggested and got out a big pot.

"Thanks, Emma. That will be great."

"What game are you going to play?" I asked, as I poured a cup of corn into a big pot.

"Poker," he said with a devilish grin.

"Are you any good at it?" I had a feeling he was.

"Not at all," he said with the innocent voice of a child. "Do I look like a kid that knows how to play such a grown-up game?" I thought I might want to go to game night now, just to watch Ivar shark the crew at cards.

"Be careful. If they throw you overboard, you might not make the swim back to Tahiti."

Ivar was good at poker, but he underestimated the puny mortals he was playing. He even got caught cheating, which didn't go over very well with the crew, and they banned him from the poker table.

"You can play Yahtzee with me if you want." Ivar plopped himself down in the chair next to me, and he looked very much like your typical broody teenager. "Do you always cheat at cards?" I asked him to try and lighten his mood.

"Only when I'm not winning." Ivar leaned in and scowled at the men playing poker.

"Can you teach me how to cheat at cards?" I asked him. Ivar straightened up and looked at me, then said with sincerity.

"It would be an honor." He grabbed a deck from his pocket and said, "Let's start with the false cut."

I took a quick look at the crew at the other table and then leaned in to quietly talk with Ivar without being overheard. "They all act so normal. They picked up a half-naked man from Antarctica. Don't they think that's strange?"

Ivar stopped shuffling the cards and pointed at Richie, "He was kicked out of the Navy for claiming aliens abducted him. If he starts talking about immortal men in Antarctica, what do you think his doctors will do to him? The captain believes in curses and doesn't want to bring any black magic down on his family, so he would never say a word. Those two guys grew up in the Turkish mafia. We pay everyone enough to keep their mouth shut. Your cook buddy, Svetlana? Ex KGB." I thought Ivar was pulling my leg for a second, but he was serious as he started dealing the cards. "Now pay attention, see how I'm actually dealing you the second card from the top of the deck? Here let me slow it down for you."

That night I laid in bed and imagined a young femme-fatal Svetlana wearing poisoned red lipstick and a gun strapped to her thigh. And Richie, did he really see aliens? Anything was possible now. Immortal Vikings, a lake monster, I had just helped kill Dracula less than a week ago. The thought of Ivan the Terrible caught me off guard. I felt the memory flashback with each beat of my heart. The wet metal cage in the ship's artificial light. His white body, being pulled out by Bjorn. The way his skin felt. How black his eyes were. The piece of heart in my hand, like a peach pit. His kick to my chest. I was drowning. I was dying.

Filling my lungs with air, I took a deep breath to prove to myself I still could and sat up in bed. It was time to fix Svetlana's sweater, right now, I decided. It would be a good distraction, something I could focus on that was real and now. While I was sewing the hole in Svetlana's sweater, I noticed that it smelled, so I decided I'd wash it too. Since I was going to wash her sweater, I thought I'd wash her leggings, socks, my apron, and underwear as well. So, I bundled everything into my pillowcase because it could use a wash too. *How did the crew do laundry on the ship?* Besides handwashing my only pair of underwear when I showered, I hadn't thought about doing laundry. I decided to use the galley sink for this project. Filling a little warm water in the sink with some dish soap, I began to slosh the clothes around with my hands. The water turned dark grey; I just kept sloshing the clothes around and rubbing the bits that had stains on them. Then, I unplugged the drain and tried to wring out the clothes, but my hands weren't very strong. So, I took off my shoes, climbed into the sink, and started stepping on the wet clothes, squishing out the dirty, sudsy water. That's when Bjorn walked by and did a double take.

"What's going on in here?" he asked.

"Laundry?" My answer sounded more like a question.

"Would you mind doing mine next?"

"Sure, okay." Why not? I thought this was fun. I filled the sink with some clean water and stomped around a bit more for the rinse cycle.

The problem I ran into was what to do with the wet clothes after washing them. I hung Svetlana's sweater on its coat hanger and hung it over the showerhead in the latrine. It was still dripping, and I wondered if it would take days to dry and end up smelling even worse than when it was dirty. The leggings were a synthetic material and felt like they would be dry overnight. I was worried about her socks too. I think they might have shrunk a little. I began pulling on them to stretch them out again and hung the pillowcase and apron in the galley. My underwear I put over my doorknob in my quarters.

"Sorry, I didn't think the drying part through," I said, as I handed Bjorn his sopping wet, slightly cleaner laundry.

Thanks to the extra energy I used on doing laundry, I slept blissfully, without dreaming, and woke up feeling great. I yawned and stretched my body out, flexing every muscle, and then I remembered my rib and stopped halfway through the stretch. Cautiously, I stretched my side, but it didn't hurt. Thinking back, it didn't hurt yesterday, either. That's lucky, I must not have hurt it so badly after all.

Between meals, I spent my extra time on deck. I had been couped up below in the galley for days, and I longed for some fresh air now that it wasn't unbearably cold anymore. It was still chilly, but it felt good, refreshing. Like the end of autumn right before the beginning of winter. The days were still short, but the moments of sunshine I did find, I would soak up with delight.

"What a beautiful feeling," I said aloud to myself, thinking that I was alone. So, I was startled when I heard a reply.

"Yes, it is wonderful. Life tastes much better when there is less of it. The simplest moments become a delicacy." Ragnar stood just behind me, holding a massive-looking fishing pole. He was still wearing Bjorn's turtleneck, which he had adorned with several different fishing hooks on the sleeve, and he was still barefoot.

"Aren't your feet cold?" I asked.

"Aren't your feet hot?" he replied and looked down at my doubled-up socks and heavy boots. Ragnar smoothed out his beard with his free hand and took a deep breath with his eyes closed and wiggled his toes. Now that I was thinking about it, my feet did feel kind of hot.

"What do you think will happen at the thing?" I asked, as I watched him pluck a hook from his sleeve and began to tie it onto his fishing line.

"Everyone will have a chance to speak. I expect there will be opposition from a few men that wish to remain immortal. Sigurd will be the key to swaying them. He would never willingly admit that I am right, but I know he must be tired and growing perpetually bored with every new lifetime. So, I will let him speak first. I will listen and be the very last to speak." I thought that was an intelligent strategy. Having the last word would give him the upper hand.

"And then what?" I asked, and he looked at me confused. "Let's assume a best-case scenario. Everyone says they will give up their immortality. How do you keep them from changing their minds later? Or if they get sick. Or someone they love gets sick." I took a minute to compose myself. "What if they have regrets? The heart could cure cancer." I looked into Ragnar's fierce grey eyes and thought of my mother. "Think about what it could do for medicine; think about the lives it could save."

Ragnar looked sternly at me. "You think you would make better choices with this power? You might think you would, but I have witnessed much. Man has not changed in a thousand years. Its power would not be used to cure and treat the sick. Who would decide who was the most in need of saving, you? No, you are no god! Its powers would be bestowed to the highest bidder. The richest or the most ruthless and most powerful men in the world would take it from you. Who are you to stop them? Where is your army?" Ragnar held my shoulder with his free hand. "It is, and always will be, used as a weapon, child." He let go of me and looked out to the sea.

My eyes filled with tears; I knew he was right. What would I have given for a chance to cure my mother, to give her another chance at life? I mumbled something about making more coffee and left to go back below deck, and maybe take off my extra pair of socks.

Stopping to use the latrine, I checked on Svetlana's sweater and was relieved to find it had dried, but it felt stiff, so did her socks. I crunched them in my hands to try and soften them up a little, but it was such an awful feeling I gave up and put them back in her storage locker. I put an equally stiff pillowcase back on my pillow and tried to look out of the little port window in my room. It looked like we were slowing down. Looking around the rest of my tiny space, I focused on the little imperfections in the walls. I turned the light above my bed on and off a few times and thought about what life would be like if this were my career. "I don't know how you do it, Svetlana," I said to myself. "I am so ready to get off this ship."

Maybe Bjorn was up to something interesting, I hadn't seen him all day. He was probably sleeping, maybe I should go and wake him up. He had just begun rotating shifts with the captain, so now Bjorn was navigating the ship at night, freeing up the first mate to help with repairs caused by the last storm. I was pretty sure Ivar was on cleaning detail and would stay on cleaning detail for the stunt he pulled at the poker table. It turned out these guys take cards very seriously.

I walked to Bjorn's door and pressed my ear against it, but I couldn't hear anything. I knocked lightly and then opened it, but he wasn't there. Disappointed, I started walking back to the galley. That's when I saw him. Bjorn was heading up the steps to go above deck. "Bjorn!" I shouted, and he turned around.

"There you are, Emma. I'm borrowing a can of crab meat," he told me as he walked back toward me. "Do you like to fish? The ship's engine needs to be turned off for maintenance. Which allows us time to go fishing." Bjorn was beaming.

"I don't know, I've never tried it," I told him honestly. I grew up in the city, the closest I ever got to fishing was at the state fair, using a stick with a magnet tied to the end of a string to catch swimming ducks for a prize. I loved that game. So, I followed Bjorn above deck, excited to receive my first fishing lesson.

Bjorn wrapped his arms around me and instructed me on how to tie a *Uni knot* around the hook. He tied several of them along the line and added a big lead weight at the end to sink the line. Then, he let me put the crab meat on the hook and helped me cast the fishing line off the back of the ship, and then we waited. I soon found out my expectations of catching fish were not very realistic. I thought we would have a fish soon after casting the line, but it's a big ocean. A big empty ocean because nothing was happening.

It felt like I had stood there for an hour. *Where were all the fish?* I looked at Bjorn. He and his father seemed completely content, just staring at the ocean as if this was normal. "Wow, look at the time. Thanks, this was great, but I've got to get back to work. Come get me if you catch anything." I hugged Bjorn and waved goodbye to Ragnar as I left to go and find something, anything, to do that wasn't fishing.

The ship began to move again shortly after dark. Bjorn and Ragnar ended up not catching anything. *What a waste of a can of crab meat*, I thought, as I finished preparing dinner.

The ship seemed to go faster after the repairs. Or maybe it just felt like it compared to being adrift most of the day. I finished cleaning up and thought about how fast the week had gone. It had only been a week ago that I nearly drowned and just two weeks ago since I was almost culled. I saw Ivar walk by the galley with a mop. "Ivar? You want to finish the last of the ice cream with me?"

Ivar walked backwards into view, smiling. "I'll grab the spoons and the cartons and meet you in the common area. Can you mop my floor for me really quickly?"

I brought everything to the common room and turned on the computer. I felt like I should do some homework on the Viking clan before the thing, so I searched for a documentary on Vikings. There was one about Ivar, and I clicked play just as Ivar joined me. I handed him a big spoon and a nearly empty carton of cookies and cream ice cream because I was going to finish the chocolate.

"What are we watching?" Ivar asked, as he settled into a chair next to me.

"I thought you could help me with some homework," I said, as the documentary began.

"Hey, that's Alt Clud!" Ivar said, as the narrator started talking about a fortress on a rock in Glasgow. "Is this documentary about me?" He put his feet up on the desk and grinned between big spoonsful of ice cream. "Here they go with the boneless crap again." Ivar scowled and scrapped the last spoon of ice cream out of his carton. I handed him mine, and he grunted thanks.

"I've been thinking about how I almost died last week and the week before," I confessed to Ivar.

He shrugged his shoulders. "But you didn't. Bjorn has always been good at picking survivors. That's why he claimed you. He saw a fox, not a hen." Ivar said, as he watched the documentary. I hadn't given much thought to why I was spared. I thought back on my impulse to fight as I stabbed Ivar in the neck with the letter opener. It horrified me thinking back at what I had done.

So, it was a blind fit of rage that saved my life that night and dumb luck I missed the final toast. "The toast," I remembered and asked Ivar, "what kind of poison did you use?" Ivar looked at me for a second and then got up and paused the documentary. He typed something into the search engine.

"I like documentaries too," he said and clicked play on something new. The narrator began talking about the pufferfish. Ivar leaned in and said, "Tetrodotoxin, crazy stuff, over a thousand times more poisonous than cyanide. I add lysergic acid diethylamide, LSD." Ivar finished the last spoonful of the second carton of ice cream. "It's better than the old way. The running, the screaming, the begging, and the mess." Ivar got up and stretched his stomach. "I hated the mess." He looked over his shoulder at the mop and bucket. "I should get back to swabbing the deck. It's been fun, thanks, Emma."

Death by pufferfish poison laced with LSD, I thought, as I laid down in my bed. I would prefer that to drowning. I hugged my pillow, and tears began to leak from my eyes. "You are a survivor," I whispered to myself and hugged the pillow tighter.

A few days later, Captain Youssef came down to the galley to tell me the good news. "We will be arriving at your destination late tonight. I wanted to take this opportunity to thank you for all of your hard work." He shook my hand. It felt nice to be appreciated.

"No, thank you! You saved my life. I'm, I—" I had to take a moment and clear my throat. I couldn't think of the words. So instead, I said. "I think I'll make Svetlana a welcome home cake," I told him.

"I think she would like that very much, Emma." He placed his second hand on top of mine and kissed both my cheeks and uttered another blessing. Then, he went back above deck. *What a wonderful man*, I thought, and I wondered if I could remember the cake recipe I had used for Richie's birthday. This time I was skipping the buttercream frosting.

Bjorn and Ragnar had been arguing for days. They called it debating, but it was more of a shouting match, in my opinion. They were trying to perfect their case for the thing by anticipating what everyone would say. But unfortunately, they couldn't agree on who was most likely to say what. "Your head has been on the ice too long, old man!" Bjorn was shouting at his father.

"You'll see, he only shows you half of his true nature because you are his king! I know what he says behind your back. Your overconfidence in him is a weakness!" I heard Ragnar retort back as they walked by the galley. Everyone, including me, kept their distance from the debating duo, especially Ivar, since they were trying to make him be the tiebreaker.

After I finished dinner, I took extra care to clean the galley. I wanted to leave it just as nice as Svetlana had left it for me. I set the cake on the counter and decided I should write a note. *Dear Svetlana*, I began the message on the back of a new Yahtzee scorecard and then drew a total blank as to what I should write next. I was horrible at writing notes. I wanted to come up with something funny and cute, but all I could do was stare at the space on the paper. *I'm sorry about the laundry.* I wrote, and I really was. Then, I drew a heart and wrote my name. "Well, it's the thought that counts," I said to myself. I hung up my apron and took one last look at the galley and turned the lights off.

I had already changed into my dress, so I grabbed my shawl and toiletry bag and went outside to see if I could spot land yet. It was a clear night, and a full moon was rising over the water. I watched as its yellow light danced on the surface and thought how lucky I was to have witnessed such a beautiful moment. I also realized how lonely I was. I wanted to share the moonrise with Bjorn. I watched the stars and the moon, breathed in the fresh air, and thought about what my future might look like. Bjorn said he'd show me the world. Maybe we could go to Africa next. I'd read about a hotel where you could feed giraffes from the windows at breakfast. And I wondered if I should pick a new name. I'd need a new passport, so why not choose a new name? Maybe, Emily, it's close to Emma, or Amelia. Or maybe Bjorn had already thought of that. He had introduced me to the crew as Emma Lodbrok. It would be simpler to keep my first name and just change my last to his.

The ship's horn blew, I didn't even know the ship had a horn. It startled me so badly, I felt like my heart had tried to jump out of my chest. The entire crew came out onto the deck, and Ragnar shouted, "Land ho," as he slapped Bjorn and Ivar on their backs.

I looked out to the water in confusion. I still didn't see anything, but then I realized I had simply been looking from the wrong side of the *Bryony*. I walked over to the other side of the ship, and there it was, the orange glow of fires on the beach, but the windows of the resort were all black, making the building seem nearly invisible. "Land ho," I whispered to myself and went to stand next to Bjorn.

Soon there was a familiar voice below the ship on the water's edge. "Four to come aboard!" Svetlana called out from the rowboat. Richie lowered the ladder and up popped Svetlana's sun-kissed smiling face. The crew embraced and welcomed each other back. Svetlana had brought a crate of fresh fruit and fish from the island, which some of the crew members seemed especially excited about as they carried it to the galley for her.

"Svetlana, look at you. You look amazing. How was your R&R?" I asked her while we hugged.

"It was so good, but you know, I think I need vacation from vacation. I drank too much and slept too little," she said, as she held her head for dramatic effect. I gave her back her locker key, and she hugged me one last time before it was my turn to climb down the ladder.

No one said anything about Ragnar. They didn't even look at him. Either they weren't surprised, or they just had good poker faces. Finally, it was time to go—what a bittersweet feeling. I began to climb down into the rowboat but stopped to blow everyone a kiss and took one last look at the *Bryony* and her crew.

¤ *The Decision* ¤

My knees were shaking as I climbed down the ladder. They continued to shake the entire boat ride back to the island. Bjorn and Ragnar were still arguing as Ivar rowed, but in their language. I wondered why they made the switch from English. I began to feel like maybe they were talking about me. A lump was growing in my throat. I wrapped my shawl tighter around my shoulders and took my shoes off. I didn't want to get them wet when it was time to jump from the boat.

Ivar launched the rowboat onto the shore with one last mighty stroke where it came to a sudden, grinding stop. He jumped out first, and I climbed over his seat and jumped next. Bjorn and Ragnar finally stopped arguing and jumped off the sides of the boat and picked it up. They carried it further up the shore so the tide wouldn't catch it.

Sigurd was waiting for us. He was holding the white horn I had seen Ivar blow for the culling. I began to tremble just looking at it. "Brothers!" He greeted Bjorn and Ivar with an outstretched arm. They both grabbed Sigurd and embraced him warmly. "Welcome back. I'm looking forward to hearing about your journey." Sigurd then extended his arm to Ragnar. "Father?" he said cautiously. Ragnar ignored his arm and began to walk up the beach.

"What do they know?" That was all he said to his son.

"Nothing. They are all very curious why a thing has been called." Sigurd answered his father as he followed behind him.

"But you know," Ragnar stopped and looked at Sigurd pointedly. "And you claim you told no one?" Sigurd looked defensively at his father.

"You will believe what you want to believe. You always have. But I kept my word to Bjorn and have not uttered a word." Ragnar just looked at him and then spat on the ground. Bjorn and Ivar ignored them both and kept on walking. There was a fire up ahead, so I followed them, and eventually, so did Ragnar and Sigurd.

It felt strange walking on the wet beach. The ground felt as though it was still swaying below my feet. When I reached the fire, I noticed a large circle was drawn around it in the sand. Inside the circle, there was only one chair, a fold-up chair with a drink holder. Bjorn went and sat in it. "Call them, brother!" he ordered Sigurd, who took a deep breath and blew a hollow ominous tune from the horn. Ivar knelt to the right of Bjorn, and Ragnar sat to Bjorn's left.

After Sigurd had finished blowing the horn, he looked at me and said, "Emma, you may stand outside of the circle." So that's what I did. I stood alone outside of the sand circle, in the dark, trembling, but not from cold, as I watched the young immortal Vikings arrive and fill the inner circle around the fire. Some of them looked surprised to see me as they passed by and took their places.

"That's right, assholes, I'm still alive," I whispered to myself through my teeth.

When everyone had taken their places, Bjorn nodded to Ivar, who then stood and walked closer to the fire. All eyes were on him as he took the same small knife he had found in the galley and cut it into his hand. Then, he held up his bloody palm for all to see as blood began to drip down his arm and onto the sand. My view was swallowed up as everyone stood and began shouting a frenzy of questions. They didn't sit down again until Ivar had gone around to each man and let them inspect his wound. Some of the men began sobbing and dropped to their knees. I couldn't see Ragnar, but I was sure he was paying close attention to everyone's reactions. Then, as if a signal had been given, everyone sat down and became quiet. That's when I saw Bjorn standing with his fist in the air. He put his arm down and took a step toward the fire.

"Now listen, and your questions will become answered," Bjorn said in a normal speaking voice.

Besides the crackling of the fire and the insects of the night, there was no other noise. He had his audience at full attention.

"A parasite lives inside of us. We took it into our bodies not knowing the consequences. This parasite still lives." Bjorn looked around at his men. "And it can be removed." The men began to express mumbles of excitement. "Ivar has shown you, it is not us that is immortal, rather it's the parasite that gives us our powers. Without it, we are flesh and blood; we are still mortal men. And now we can finally live with honor, and we can finally die with honor!"

That last statement was like a Viking home run. All the men had stood up again and were shouting and cheering for their king and his good news. When they settled down again, Sigurd stood close to the fire with his fist in the air. Ragnar looked pleased as Sigurd lowered his hand and began to speak.

"Hearsay and half-truths!" Sigurd shouted at Bjorn. Some in the crowd began to hiss at Sigurd like a snake. "It is the heart of the water horse that has been giving us our powers, if anything, we are the parasite, leaching off its immortality and thinking it was our own. Look, it still beats!" Sigurd held out his hand and showed the fleshy bite of the beast's heart, which glistened in the moonlight.

"Trickery!" Someone in the circle shouted.

Bjorn stood. "Silence!" he ordered, then sat again and let Sigurd continue.

"What I hold in my hand is a weapon. One we have a responsibility to keep from the outside world. We must stay brave." Sigurd looked at his hand and then swallowed the piece of heart.

"The burden is ours. Forever." I looked at the reaction of the men, and several seemed to agree with Sigurd.

Then, Ragnar stood with his fist raised in the air, and the men became still again as Sigurd took his seat. "Carrying this burden does not make us honorable men; those who cannot die in battle cannot be called brave. You are cowards and cheats!" He pointed at some of the men that moments ago seemed to agree with Sigurd. "Addicted to the power you hold, over death herself. We have cast ourselves out of Valhalla for eternity." Ragnar looked at Sigurd and spat on the ground. "You play at being a god," he accused him. "But we are not gods! We are the giants we have sworn to destroy!"

Ragnar beat his hands on his chest, and the men began to do the same in a crazed frenzy as they stood back up on their feet. It took a much longer time for them to settle down again. Ragnar was still standing with his fist in the air.

"But Sigurd speaks an important truth," he continued. "It is a weapon, one that is too powerful for even us to wield any longer. Now we have been given a choice, we must choose to be free of such corruption. And sink this curse to the bottom of the ocean!" It looked like all the men had reached the same conclusion as Ragnar, just like he wanted them to. Even Sigurd appeared to agree with his father.

So, why I was pushing my way through to the inner circle with my fist raised in the air, still clutching my sandals in my other hand, wasn't exactly clear to me until I was there. Everyone was looking at me like I was a pariah, but I stood anyway with my fist trembling until Bjorn gave a little wave of approval, and the men all sat down and let me speak. "Sigurd was right. You need a guardian! But he was wrong about who it should be. As Ragnar said, it's too dangerous to be left to any of you. So, give it *back*." My voice began to break. I was still shaking, but this time not from nerves but from anger. "Give it back to the beast you stole it from in the first place! You cowards," I said angrily, because at that moment, all I could think about was how these men had trapped her. They had cut into her with their axes so many years ago to rob her of her power.

Then, in a blink, my anger was gone as I looked around and saw scared boys going to battle. In a time that convinced them they were men, and they believed the lies their kings told them. That to die in battle was glorious.

"I'm sorry. You didn't know this would happen to you. Now you have a choice, that's what it should be. *Your* choice, but I think you've already made it. Long before any of us spoke tonight." I put my fist down. The men were silent. Popping noises from the fire made me jump. I looked at Bjorn's face, his was unreadable, but Ragnar looked livid.

Bjorn put his hands on his knees, "Does anyone else want to speak?" He paused for a moment to look at all his men, but none of them stood. "Then we vote," he declared. Ragnar stood up on the opposite side of the fire from me. Sigurd stood to form a triangle, but he looked at me and then his father, then walked to stand by my side.

"Anything's better than having to agree with that warthog. My vote is with you," he whispered and grinned at his father.

I felt my shoulders relax a little. "I thought you were coming over here to tell me to sit down," I confessed to him.

One of the men stood and came to stand by my other side. He had dark hair and was taller than the other men. "One last epic quest," the man said proudly.

"Aren't you afraid the beast might eat you?" said another, as he came to stand by me.

"No, I'm all skin and bones, but we might throw you to the beast as a peace offering," retorted the first and poked the other man in his meaty belly.

All the men stood, and every single one of them came to stand on my side of the fire. Bjorn stayed seated, but Ivar came over to me and whispered in my ear, "Clever fox. It looks like you live another day." What did he mean by that? I wanted to ask him, but Ragnar had walked over to me with his hand out. I took it, and he squeezed a little harder than he needed to.

"We all want the same thing," he said loudly so the entire group could hear him. "Let us celebrate!" he added, as he let go of my hand.

Bjorn stood up and kicked the sand circle to break it symbolically. "The decision is made! Let us discuss the course less formally." He bellowed with excitement in his voice. The rest of his men copied his enthusiasm, and the small fire quickly became a bonfire as huge chunks of driftwood were placed on top of it. Sometimes the growing flames turned blue from the salt in the wood.

The men gathered around Ivar, who took a seat in Bjorn's chair. Drinks in hand, they listened to the recent events of his transition to mortal during our Arctic journey. "It will most likely be healed by the morning." Ivar held out his hand for the men to see again. "But the effects are waning. I even got seasick," he boasted.

"And he's hungry all the time," Bjorn added, as he threw Ivar an orange.

"Bjorn, tell us of the prisoner," said Sigurd, and the men grew tense.

"The devil is back in hell. We were able to take his piece of the heart," Bjorn said, and the tension from the men lifted. "But we lost it to the ocean," Bjorn continued, and some of the men began to look uncomfortable.

Ivar took up his story again, describing the feeling of throwing up. "Hand me a beer. I haven't tried to get drunk yet." Ivar seemed excited that he had a new experiment to put himself through.

Bjorn walked over to me, and I leaned into him. "Are you worried the guests will be attracted to the bonfire?" Bjorn took my arm and started walking with me to the resort.

"It's off season, our last event was Viking Palooza. So, we are officially closed until spring for renovations."

I cleared my throat and asked him, "On the rowboat, were you and your father arguing about me? Sorry, I'm silly. I just had the most paranoid idea that—"

"That we were arguing about if we should kill you or not?" Bjorn looked at me, winked, and laughed. Was he joking? I laughed with him and thought, *Of course, Bjorn's joking.* But then I thought about the look on Ragnar's face when he saw me enter the circle, and I wasn't so sure. "Let's go check the lost and found, maybe we can find you some new clothes." Bjorn looked at me hopeful.

"And a *shower*," I said the word slowly. "One I can leave on the whole time, and a washing machine and a dryer?" I was visibly giddy as we walked arm and arm into the resort through the front doors. "Jackpot!" I exclaimed, as I dug through all the left-behind belongings.

I found a wrap skirt and a pair of designer sunglasses. I also found some leggings and several tank tops that fit me. There were even a couple of pairs of lacey underwear. I thought after a good wash, why not. I also found my shorts and shirt that had been rolled up in the towel in Bjorn's bathroom. And I took a man's t-shirt, it smelled strongly of cologne, but I thought it would make a great nightshirt. Bjorn brought me a room key and told me where the laundry room was.

"I need to work out some travel arrangements, will you be okay without me for tonight?" I nodded as Bjorn took both of my hands and kissed them.

"You did so well tonight, Emma. The look on my father's face when you entered the circle," Bjorn let out a loud laugh, "and then when everyone voted with you, I had to bite my cheek to keep from laughing." He wiped a tear from his eyes and began to walk out the front door.

"Bjorn?" I called after him. "I'll need a few more things I can't get from the lost and found."

Bjorn smiled at me. "Of course, make a list and give it to Ivar." He blew me a kiss and continued out the door back to the bonfire.

ÁSATRÚARFÉLAGIÐ
¤ *High Priest* ¤

My room had a single bed with all-white bedding and a nightstand on each side. The hardwood floor was accented with a large grass mat. A big round fan attached to the corner of the wall sat next to the mounted flat screen, and long white curtains hung down around the window. The room felt so big after spending the last couple of weeks in the ship's tiny quarters. I undressed in the middle of my room and ran straight for the shower. It was an open shower with smooth stones on the floor. The walls were tiled with rougher stones, and there was a little hook holding a grass basket filled with shower goodies. Shampoo, soap, shower cap, even a locally made lemongrass sugar scrub.

I didn't get a sugar scrub in my old room, I thought. Then again, this room was much nicer than the first one I stayed. The second floor had carpeting and older-looking bathrooms. *Maybe that's what they were going to renovate during the offseason*, I thought, as I turned on the water. Then, all thoughts washed away as pure bliss filled me.

"Oh my God!" I moaned, as the shower hit my head and shoulders. I couldn't wait to wash the smell of the ship and smoke from the bonfire out of my hair. The suds slipped down my back and into the drain. I had taken showers for granted up to this point in my life. This was luxury, and I understood that now.

After my shower, I wrapped my body in an oversized, soft towel and began to pat dry my hair. Now that I was clean, I could smell how badly my clothes reeked of the ship, smoke, and body odor.

I bundled everything up with my lost and found treasures and headed to the laundry room. There were two big industrial washing machines and four smaller regular-looking machines. I put everything together in one of the smaller machines, added a big scoop of laundry detergent, and started the machine. In the corner of the room were stacks of clean folded towels and fresh sheets. I grabbed a few extra towels just because I could and started walking back to my room.

Being alone in the hallway made me think of the last time I had been here. When I reached my room, I wasn't ready to go in it yet. I felt like I had unfinished business to attend to, so I kept walking to the door with the staff-only sign. This time it was unlocked, so I opened the door and looked at the kitchen, expecting something to be left behind. There must be some evidence or sign of a struggle, like a drop of blood that wasn't cleaned up, but there was nothing. I wondered where the staff had been during all of this. Had it only been Bjorn's men working here? I tried to remember, but I hadn't paid attention before. No, someone else had given me my room key. There must have been others, too, at least during the day shift.

I left the kitchen and kept walking down the hall to the courtyard. The last time I had been there it was full of dead bodies, and I didn't want that image to haunt me for the rest of my life. I had to see the courtyard, empty and clean. Not to erase the memory of what happened, but to try and move on. My feet froze at the very edge of the hallway right before I could step out onto the courtyard. *I don't think I can go any further.* The courtyard was empty, I had come to see what I needed to, but I couldn't bring myself to step out into it.

"I'm sorry," I whispered to the ghosts. "I should've been with you." A gust of wind came up from the courtyard and blew on my face. A tear ran down my cheek, and as strange as it may sound, I somehow felt forgiven, that Rachel was not angry at me for surviving. "Thank you," I whispered back to the wind. I turned and walked back down the hall, only pausing briefly at the hidden door. Then, I went back to my room and locked it with the bolt.

While waiting for my laundry to finish, I blow-dried my hair and started writing my list of things I'd need. There was a pen and paper pad on the nightstand. I looked at my hairy legs. "Emma, you're a werewolf!" I laughed and howled, after all, it was a full moon. I put shaving razors as my first item.

I also didn't want to be caught without pads just in case my period did start. So, I wrote down the name brand I liked and absorbency strength to make sure Ivar got the right ones. Then, I put down my clothing and shoe sizes, and I remembered I desperately wanted lip balm, putting a big exclamation mark next to it on the notepad. I also wanted a pack of new underwear, the granny-style ones, and added a note to make sure they were cotton. I didn't want to have to be stuck with lacey butt floss for the rest of the week. My list was a little embarrassing, but I reminded myself Ivar was over a thousand years old, not a kid, even if he looked like one. He could handle buying me menstrual pads and granny panties. I put the pen down and decided to check on my laundry. Retightening the towel around myself, I unbolted the door and walked to the laundry room. The washing machine was on the spin cycle.

While I waited, I looked through the cabinets in the laundry room. There were cleaning supplies and toilet paper. Then, I found the exciting cabinet with the mini soaps and shampoos. There were also razors and shaving cream, lip balms, deodorant, toothbrushes, toothpaste, floss, mouthwash, sewing kits, shower caps, slippers, lotions, sugar scrub, condoms, feminine pads, and even baby diapers. "Um, yes, please, I'll take one of you and you, and come here you," I said as I loaded up my hands with goodies.

I opened a lip balm and slathered it on my lips. *Mm, mint, I love mint.* The washing machine stopped spinning, and I switched everything over to the dryer. I filled a pillowcase with my loot, put on a pair of slippers, and went back to my room to shave my legs and redo my list.

I'm so shiny, I thought, as I laid back on my bed and admired my freshly shaved legs. It felt so good to be washed, scrubbed, and polished. It should be about time to check on the dryer. Wearing just a towel was getting uncomfortable. So, I got up and put my slippers back on, but instead of going straight to the laundry room, I thought I'd take a detour to the kitchen and liberate a bottle of champagne. The kitchen had an entire refrigerator filled with all different kinds of wines and champagnes. It was like an adult vending machine; I grabbed a bottle and a glass and went to check on my clothes.

It looked like the dryer had been done for a while. My wrap skirt was wrinkly, but everything else looked fine. I slipped into the t-shirt, it was warm and still smelled faintly of the last owner's cologne. The laundry room had a commercial ironing press used for sheets in the corner. *Why not*, I thought, so I plugged it in. After a minute, I could smell it was hot. I spread out my wrap skirt and let the roller take it. My wrap skirt came out the other end perfectly pressed. I unplugged the machine and folded my clothes nicer than I usually would have and took everything back to my room.

Putting a hand towel over the champagne cork and the bottle between my legs, I pulled and wiggled until, *pop!* What an exciting sound. I poured myself a glass and held it up to the light, admiring the bubbles. "Looks like I finally got around to that last toast. Here's to you, Rachel, and you, mom. It's taken longer than I thought it would, but I've started living my best life." The words felt like they were choking me, so I stopped talking and took a sip. I walked over to the window, but it was too dark to see anything, so I sat down on my bed with the T.V. remote and browsed the channels while drinking my bubble juice. Unfortunately, there wasn't much on. Wow, a lot of late-night T.V. seemed to just be porn.

Pouring myself another glass of champagne, I realized I'd almost drank the entire bottle. Usually, I was a real lightweight when it came to drinking. I'd practically just have to sniff the cork and I'd begin to feel tipsy. Rubbing my face, it felt numb. "Yep, stick a fork in you. 'Cause you're done." It was *past* time to go to bed. I sat the almost full glass down, turned off the T.V., and realized I *really* had to go pee. I took my new complimentary toothbrush and toothpaste and brushed my teeth for what felt like an obscenely long time, it just felt so good. I swished my mouth out with water and took a drink straight from the faucet. Then, I turned off the light and fell face-first into bed.

¤ ¤ ¤

"Bjorn, what are you doing here?" Bjorn was standing, looking out my window, the white curtains were billowing around him.

"Sorry, Emma, I didn't mean to scare you. Can I sleep here tonight?"

I nodded, "Sure, but you have to take a shower first. You smell like bonfire smoke."

He smiled and kissed my neck. "Only if you take one with me." He picked me up from bed. The rocks were rough against my back as Bjorn pressed himself against me. I began to shampoo his hard cock, and he moaned and moved his fingers down my wet body, in between my legs.

"Do you hear something?" he asked.

What was that knocking noise?

¤ ¤ ¤

The shower and Bjorn disappeared as I woke up and looked around. I was alone in bed, and the sun was shining through my window. Someone was knocking on the door. "No! Go away," I took my pillow and pressed it into my face.

"Emma. If you want me to go shopping for you, I need you to give me your list. Now!" It was Ivar, I crawled out of bed and grabbed my list, opened the door, and held it out for him.

"Wow, Ivar, you look awful," I couldn't help but notice.

"He can't drink like a fish anymore," said the man standing next to him. He had on a white linen shirt. His bleach blond hair with slightly dark roots was shaved on one side with a braid along the part.

"Hi," I said, as he reached out his white-painted nails and took the list from me.

"Oh no, girl. This is just sad," he said, as he read my list. "Lucky for you, your fairy God Viking is here," and he let himself into my room. He took the pen from my dresser and began to add a few items. "There, that's the basics," he folded the list in half and handed it to Ivar, who bowed as he took it and left to run his errands.

"Did he just bow to you?" I asked my fairy God Viking, he nodded.

"I'm High Priest Hvitserk Ragnarsson. I'm a big deal, but you can call me Stacey," he squeezed my hand and turned me around as if we were dancing. "Ms. Emma, we are going to start with your hair. Do you trust me?" He didn't wait for an answer. Instead, he just went back out into the hallway and brought in a rolling, professional hair and makeup organizer and a fold-up chair. "Open the window, and good, I see you have extra towels. Now take a seat."

Stacey cut a few inches off my hair and mixed up some bleach. "We are going to add a little summer to your winter complexion," he said and started tearing foils.

"Were you at the thing?" I asked him, I didn't remember seeing him.

"Odin, no! I had far more important things to do, like my nails. Besides, I already knew how it was going to turn out. The runes told me, and yes, girl, I'll give you a reading just as soon as I finish with these foils. Alright, now let's take a peek at what the weavers are up to," Stacey took out a white satin bag and shook it in his hand. He drew out one white stone and showed it to me. It looked like a big *R*, "Your past, a journey," and he set it down in front of me, then reached his hand into the bag again and pulled out another stone. It looked like a big *X*, "Your present, a gift, that's me, girl," he laughed and put it next to the first. Then, he drew one more stone and looked at it with a frown.

"Is that one my future? It looks kind of like a thorn," I said, as I tilted my head to get a better look.

Stacey's face looked serious, "Betrayal." He put all three stones back into his bag and drew the string tight. "They are just a bunch of rocks with squiggly lines on them, what do they know," then he began brushing in my new highlights. "So, spill the tea, what's the situation with you and Bjorn?"

It was so nice to be able to talk to someone about our relationship finally. "Well, on the ship, he introduced me as Mrs. Lodbrok, and I hardly know him, but I liked the way it sounded." I could feel my cheeks getting hot.

"Did he now! Girl, did you two do the deed during those long, hard nights at sea?"

I covered my face. "That is none of your business."

Stacey laughed, "I take that as a yes. No shame in it, queen. But these nails? You should be embarrassed," he handed me a little pink tube. "Here, rub this on your cuticles and let it sit while I finish your hair, then we'll see what we can do about your nails."

Stacey helped me wash my hair out in the sink and had me put in a leave-in conditioner. I wrapped my hair in a towel, and he started on my nails. "I haven't painted my nails since I was in high school. It's not allowed where I worked." Stacey took out a bold shade of red and a super thin brush, he began painting symbols on my nails. "What's that?" I asked.

"I'm drawing protective runes on your nails. I'll cover them with a second coat. You'll only be able to see them if you look closely," he blew on one of the symbols.

The gesture touched me. "Thank you, Stacey."

My mind drifted to the water horse and if there really would be anything left to find after a thousand years. Then, I thought of petrified forests and mummies in ancient tombs and thought maybe a thousand years isn't that long. It just seemed like it to me because I didn't have perspective. Stacey pulled out a nail polish dryer and plugged it in. Then, he took the towel off my head and began to blow dry my hair. It had been a long time since someone had made me feel as pampered as Stacey had.

"And blot, this color matches your nails perfectly," Stacey said and handed me my sunglasses. "Sunglasses and lipstick. It's all you need today and every day. Go on, have a look at you."

I went and looked in the bathroom mirror. "Stacey, you are a gift," I told him while I admired his work in the mirror. "I look expensive." I felt like a completely new person.

"I will see you in a few days. Here, you keep the lipstick." Stacey picked up and began to leave.

"Do you want to raid the kitchen for some lunch before you go?" I asked him. "No, girl, I have a plane to catch." He came over and hugged me. I thought it would be a quick pat on the back, but he held me, really kept me close. The last time I was ever hugged like that was by my mom. "Guard your heart, M&M.," he whispered in my ear.

Then, he cleared his throat and left, the door slowly shut behind him, and as the latch clicked, I fell to my knees. "Mom?" I covered my mouth; my body shook as I cried painful but grateful tears.

¤ *Home Is Where the Heart Is* ¤

"Just look bored and keep your sunglasses on," Ivar whispered into my ear as Bjorn handed a stack of passports to the security guard at the airport. Bjorn had acquired a passport for me to use on short notice. "Remember, if anyone asks, your name is Elizabeth Dupont because that's the name on your passport."

I nodded, so that Ivar knew I understood. The security guard started to walk in our direction. "This isn't going to work, Ivar," I whispered, beginning to panic. But the guard hardly even looked at me.

He just checked our passports again and asked, "Did anyone give you a package to bring on the flight for them? The reason I must ask is in the past, passengers have received dangerous items such as bombs without their knowledge." He stopped and looked up at me.

"N-n-no," I stuttered.

Ivar followed my answer quickly with a *no* as well and poked his father in the ribs with his elbow, who gave a sarcastic and long, "No." That was it, he handed the passports back to Bjorn, and we could immediately board the private jet Bjorn had reserved for us.

"See, nothing to worry about," Ivar said, as he climbed the stairs. I was shocked at how easy it was. I didn't even have to take my shoes off or get patted down. I guess that was part of the price tag for flying with a private jet.

"If you don't mind me asking, how do you make this kind

of money? Is it all from the resort?" I wondered out loud and marveled at the private jet.

Bjorn settled into his seat next to me and said, "Some of it's from the resort and then there are life insurance policies. It's a great way to grow generational wealth."

Right, I thought, especially since he was inheriting his own policies. "Do you give yourself a funeral?"

Bjorn nodded, "Most of the time. No open casket, of course. Here, Emma, do you like to read during flights?" Bjorn handed me a Kindle from his bag. "We still have some time before the flight takes off. So go ahead and download whatever you want."

I downloaded every book on Scotland, Loch Ness, and the Loch Ness monster I could find. "I can't believe I'm going hunting for Nessie," I said, as I clicked checkout on my cart.

Bjorn laughed, "You might be disappointed. She's not at Loch Ness. Well, not anymore. In the fifties, the rumors of a monster in the loch started becoming mainstream. So, we decided it would be best to find the body and hide it somewhere else. It's a good thing we did. The loch is very big, but every inch of it has been scanned by a fleet of ships looking for evidence of the legendary monster." Bjorn pulled up a map on his phone. "We are going here," he pointed to a cluster of islands.

I had to squint to read the name, "Orkney Islands? That's where we are going?"

Bjorn nodded. "My mother summoned the beast into our realm. Our high priest believes this is where we can return her."

The engines in the plane began to get louder. Finally, it was our turn to use the runway, and I was so full of anticipation and excitement I didn't realize I was also full of, well, I had to pee, but it was too late. The plane was gaining speed. I quickly fastened my seat belt and squeezed the armrest, and my thighs. I was going to have to hold it until we were up in the air.

"Do you think it's safe to take my seat belt off now?" I looked around for a seat belt sign but couldn't find one.

"Hm? Oh, sure," Bjorn said while he was looking at his phone. He never even put his seat belt on. I unbuckled and hurried to the lavatory.

Flying made me nervous, and the more anxious I was, the more I felt like I had to go. The lavatory was tiny, about half the size of a commercial flight. "Well, no one is joining the mile-high club in here," I said after I closed the sliding door for a little privacy. I could pee and wash my hands at the same time if I wanted to.

I felt a little bump of turbulence and braced myself against the wall. Unfortunately, there weren't any seat belts in the toilet, so I hurried up and finished, then went straight back to my seat and nervously fumbled with my seatbelt until it clicked back together.

"You don't fly much?" Bjorn looked over at me with a slightly amused grin on his face.

"I flew to the Philippines for my grandmother's funeral, but I don't remember it. I think I was three. Then, the flight and connecting flight to Tahiti, and now this." There was another bump of turbulence, and I grabbed the armrest.

Bjorn put his hand over mine and then got up. "Let me see if I can find a parachute," he said and went to the front of the plane.

I turned my head to look for Ivar. "Is he kidding? Are you kidding, Bjorn? Is something wrong with the plane?" Bjorn came back with his hands behind his back.

"Fresh out of parachutes. The pilot used the last one. But I found this!" he said and held out a bottle of champagne and two glasses. Bjorn handed me the glasses and popped the cork, which went flying and hit a window across from him.

"Don't break the plane!" I screamed at him.

"A cork isn't going to take this bird down," Bjorn reassured me, as he poured our glasses.

"Did you see any caviar?" Ivar asked, as he walked by. "I'm starving." He began rummaging through the meal options. I turned around to see what Ragnar was doing and had an involuntary snort-laugh escape my nose. Ragnar was sprawled out on the jets couch sleeping with his mouth open and a silk sleep mask covering his eyes.

Bjorn topped my glass off, and I had drunk nearly all of it in one gulp. "Here's to you, Emma. What a gift you've turned out to be. I'm sorry if you've felt neglected lately. I've been so busy with last-minute arrangements, but I've missed you." We touched our glasses and our lips. "You can make it up to me by taking me to Africa," I told him.

"What's in Africa?" Bjorn asked curiously.

"I don't know, that's why I want to go," and I kissed him again.

The champagne helped my flight jitters. So did the fact that the seats reclined into beds. It made for a very cozy nest in the sky. I read from my Kindle and daydreamed about the upcoming adventure. And I must have fallen asleep because when I woke up, we were on the ground.

"Are we in Scotland?" I sat up and looked around.

"No, we are just refueling," Bjorn informed me. I looked out my window. It was night, and I could see people in bright orange vests walking around the plane. After watching them for a few minutes, I laid back down and fell asleep, only half-waking again when the engines roared as we began to take off.

About an hour before landing, Bjorn handed me Elizabeth Dupont's passport.

"Try and memorize your details. Getting into a country is usually a little stricter than getting out, especially with private jets. They have been cracking down on human trafficking lately."

Elizabeth was ten years younger than me, but I always thought I didn't look forty. I suppose she could pass as a cousin or maybe even a sister, but we didn't look very much alike other than our hair and skin tone.

When we landed, I was nervously going over the information in Elizabeth Dupont's passport. I had been acting the whole thing out in my head. The immigration officer was going to look at me scrupulously, then ask me when my birthday was. I would say January fifteenth, and he would ask me what year, and I would say, old enough not to have to answer that question. He would laugh and say, "Welcome to Scotland, Elizabeth Dupont."

I put my sunglasses back on as the door to the plane opened, but there wasn't an issue with immigration. Bjorn handed the passports over to someone, and when we got off the plane, they were handed back to him. It was a little disappointing.

Even though we had technically flown from winter on the island to summer in Scotland, it was still colder in Scotland the morning we landed. I walked out into the fresh air with my shawl wrapped around me and thought I was going to stick out like a cold, sore thumb dressed in a skirt and sandals. However, as we walked together with our luggage to get a rental car, it turned out what I considered cold weather, the locals felt was beach weather. They were all dressed in shorts and sandals.

"You packed me a sweater, right? And socks? And rain boots? And a rain jacket?" I asked Ivar, as we passed a cute touristy-looking clothing shop.

"Not exactly; I had limited resources." Ivar told me and I stopped walking.

"Give me money," I said and put out my hand. Ivar looked at Bjorn.

"Alright, you stay with Emma and get what she needs. We will get the car." Bjorn and Ragnar continued along their way.

"Ivar, give me your wallet. It will look strange if you pay for my clothes," he handed it over, and we walked back to the shop.

A little welcoming bell rang as I opened the door. The shop smelled like lavender, and there was a very practical-looking older redheaded woman behind the counter. She had on big glasses, but she wasn't smiling. I, on the other hand, was grinning from ear to ear.

"Welcome to The Sheep's Cottage, is there something I can help you with, hen?" she asked me from behind the counter.

"Yes, do you have any outdoor shoes?"

She came out from behind the counter and went to the back of the shop. "We've got some muckers. What's your size?"

I began to follower her. "I'm a six and a half, but I'll try a seven," I told her, as I plucked a few pairs of wool socks from a display stand.

"That's American size? Here, let's try you with a four and see how that feels."

I put a pair of wool socks on and tried on the shoes. They fit great. "Thank you. I'll take them and these." I handed her the socks. There was a gorgeous grey cashmere cape with a Celtic knot design along the edges pined together with a metal clasp displayed by the register. "And that please," I pointed to the cape.

"It's all local wool, of course, and handcrafted," she said, as she lovingly folded the cape and put it in a bag. "Might you be interested in some sheep tallow soap? It's scented with lavender, and we've got unscented too." I told her I'd take one of each, and she rang me up with the tiniest hint of a smile on her face.

When we were outside again, I gave Ivar back his wallet. And we walked to meet up with Bjorn and Ragnar. They were still waiting while the car was getting cleaned. "Something about sheep shit in the floor mats," Ragnar mumbled when Ivar asked what was taking so long. A few moments later, a young, tall, very skinny man with curly brown hair came around the corner speed-walking with keys in his hand.

"Your car is ready, sir. Thank you for being so patient. I've pulled it up for you." He walked us out and opened the trunk. "Can I help you with your bags?" he asked me.

What a sweet kid, I thought, as he took my shopping bags and loaded them into the trunk with the rest of the luggage. I thanked him and sat in the back with Ivar since Ragnar had already claimed the front seat. "So, where are we going?" I asked.

"Home," said Ivar with a contented look on his face.

"One of them, we are very fond of this one. It's by the cliffs in

Durness," Bjorn told me.

I had no idea where Durness was, and I hadn't thought to bring the Kindle with me for the ride. I preferred to look out the window anyway and daydreamed as we drove past old ruins and castles, wondering what home looked like as we passed through the country. Then, finally, we arrived at the coast, and I caught myself holding my breath at how beautiful everything was. I could catch glimpses of green coastal cliffs as we turned off the paved road and drove down a washboard, gravel road.

"It's just around the bend," Ivar said, as he pressed his head against the window to look.

Home was a two-story white stone house with a grey roof and five chimneys that stood over the cliffs. A car was parked near the entrance, and just as Bjorn turned off our rental car, the front door opened, and an older-looking woman wearing an apron waved to greet us as we got out. *She looks familiar somehow*, I thought.

"I'm so sorry for your loss, dear," the woman said to Ivar. She reached out and cupped his face, "Bless you, child. You're the spitting image of him."

Ivar looked like he might start crying. "Thank you, Rosa. My grandfather has told me a lot about you. I think he loved you very much."

Rosa took her apron and wiped at the tears that had begun to fall from her eyes. "I loved him very much too, dear. And you must be Jacob's sons." She welcomed Bjorn and Ragnar.

"Yes, and this is my wife, Emma." Bjorn introduced me.

"Welcome home, all of you. I've made you soup and sandwiches and opened the windows to let in some fresh air. If you need anything at all, I'm just down the road in town. I've left my number by the phone." Rosa stopped to look at Ivar one last time and smiled, then she got in her car and drove away. Ivar stood and watched until her car disappeared around the bend.

It was so tragically romantic. I thought about the box of photos Ivar had in Bjorn's office. "All we need is love! Rosaline 1967," I said. That's why she looked familiar.

Ivar turned around and wiped the tears from his eyes. "We met in a record store. She's still crazy for the Beetles," he told me and smiled at the memory. "Her favorite song is 'In My Life.'" But then it all became too much for Ivar, he burst into sobs and disappeared inside. As Bjorn handed me my shopping bags, I could hear music float down from a room on the second floor through the open windows.

I settled for the small guest room on the first floor. It had a beautiful antique wardrobe standing across from a narrow bed, but Bjorn told me we would only be staying one night, so I didn't bother unpacking. I did change into my new socks and mucker shoes, though. Then, I went upstairs, some of the wooden steps creaking as I stepped on them. I followed the music and knocked on Ivar's door.

"Can I come in?" I asked, as I looked down at the door's white porcelain knob. I didn't hear an answer, but I opened the door anyway.

Ivar was staring out the window, and there was an old record player next to him playing the Beetles. A stack of vinyl records was lying across the lace blanket that covered a double bed. I walked up to Ivar and looked out the window at the view with him. I knew there was nothing I could say to make him feel better. So, I just reached out, held one of his hands, and listened to the record with him as he watched over the cliffs and waves.

"Let's go eat," I told Ivar, as the music stopped playing. He nodded and started to put the record away. "I'll meet you downstairs."

Just as I reached the door, Ivar called my name, and I stopped to look up at him. "Thank you," he said. He looked so old as he spoke those words. I nodded and went downstairs.

Bjorn and Ragnar had already eaten by the looks of the dirty dishes on the table. I collected them up and gave them a quick wash in the sink to reuse for Ivar and myself. We ate in silence, and the house seemed very quiet.

"Did Bjorn and Ragnar leave?" I asked.

"I think so. They probably went to start clearing the cave entrance to the beast's grave. We might hear explosions depending on how the winds blowing." I stopped eating and listened for a few seconds, but I didn't hear anything.

"What did she look like when you moved the water horse from the loch?"

Ivar finished his mouthful and then answered. "It was the strangest thing, she looked like a carved dragon you'd see on furniture or something. Perfectly detailed with her eyes closed and the jagged wound marks in her chest looked like when you break a stick in half, all rough and splintered." He picked up his bowl to drink the last of the soup out of it. Just then, I heard a distant *boom*. "Sounds like you'll be seeing for yourself soon."

It was dusk, the sun had just set at ten p.m., and Bjorn and Ragnar still hadn't come back from the cave. *Maybe the beast ate them*, I thought, as I laid in bed reading from the Kindle, but just then, I heard someone pull up in the driveway. I looked out of my window and saw a moving truck, and as I watched the driver jump down from the cab, I recognized him.

"Ivar, Sigurd is here!" I shouted, as I jumped out of bed to get the door for him.

HERROUATH
Harray Loch

Ivar went to get kerosene lanterns from his shed. I changed into my leggings and wrapped my grey cashmere cloak around my shoulders. I was so glad I had comfortable outdoor shoes, as I met Ivar and Sigurd outside. They were filling and lighting the lanterns, and Sigurd had a folded plastic tarp tucked under his arm. We followed Ivar single file as he led us through the dark toward the cliffs. All I could hear was the ocean and our footsteps.

"Are you worried someone might see our lights?" I whispered and looked around.

"I'm more worried I'll fall off a cliff!" Ivar said loudly back to me, and Sigurd laughed.

In the distance, I could see a faint light wave at us. Ivar waved his lantern back, and we began to walk faster toward it. When we reached the light, I discovered it was Bjorn with a flashlight. He was sitting on the ground, and he looked exhausted. His shirt was torn, and he was covered in sweat and dirt.

"Good of you to finally join us, brother. Now the hard part is done." Bjorn stood and handed Ivar a rope.

Ivar casually walked over the edge of the cliff. I let out a gasp and ran over to the edge, but when I cautiously looked over, I realized there was a lip on the ridge, maybe ten feet down, with an opening to a cave.

I heard Ragnar and Ivar grunt, and something slid across

the rock.

"Back up, Emma," Bjorn ordered. A moment later, one end of the rope came flying up onto the ground, and Bjorn grabbed it quickly before it could slide back off the cliff. Sigurd was helping Ivar and Ragnar as they climbed back up. Then, they all grabbed hold of the rope and began to pull. I ran over to the end of the rope and helped. With a big grunt and a mighty pull, we lifted a black mound over the lip of the cliff and onto solid ground.

I took my lantern and walked over to it. *She's smaller than I thought she would be, about the size of an average living room couch*, I thought. I held the light up close. She did look like she was carved out of black wood. I could see long, sharp scales covering her and a long, strong, flat tail like a sea snake wrapped around her body. She had legs with webbed feet tucked in tightly and a gapping shattered wound in her chest. When I got to her face, I touched her head and ran my fingers along what almost looked like feathers around her closed eyes. "We're taking you home," I whispered to her.

The men began to wrap her in the tarp. "Emma, you carry the head," Bjorn said, and we all lifted her and began to carry her back to the house. About halfway there, my hands and arms were hurting.

"Can we take a break?" I asked.

"Push through, Emma. It's only a few minutes more," Ivar told me.

"I can't believe you don't have a tractor or something," I growled back, as we kept walking.

"Come on, we're more than halfway now. The pain won't kill you," Ivar paused, "even if you wish it would."

Bjorn gave an exaggerated groan, "Enough moaning about Rosa already." Sigurd's ears perked up.

"You saw Rosaline?" he asked Ivar.

"For the love of, don't get him started!" Ragnar shouted at Sigurd. We walked the rest of the way in silence, but I could hear the occasional sniffle and quiet sob coming from Ivar.

When we got back, Sigurd let go of the beast and opened the back of the moving truck. My knees were shaking, and my hands felt like they were on fire. *Just another minute*, I told myself. We pushed her into the truck, and I could finally let go.

"Alright, Ivar, are you ready to hit the road?" Sigurd asked, as he put a lock on the sliding door.

"Let me pack you up some sandwiches," I said and went into the house to grab the last of the sandwiches Rosa made. I started looking through the drawers for a bag or something to put them in, but Ivar came behind me and pulled down an old metal lunch box from the top of the refrigerator. It had the name Jacob engraved by the latch. I took the box from him and filled it with the sandwiches. There was a thermos inside. "Do you want me to fill this with soup?"

"Yes, I don't know when I'll get to taste Rosa's cooking again."

I watched from the front steps. Ivar loaded up a few more things into the truck, and Sigurd locked it again before they drove off. Bjorn stood next to me. He had taken his shirt off and was wiping his hands and face with it.

"Do you want a bath?" I asked.

Bjorn looked at me and smiled, "Will you be giving it to me?" I smiled back as I took his hand and led him inside and upstairs to a big bathroom with a clawfoot bathtub.

"Lavender or unscented?" I asked, as I started the water.

"Lavender," Bjorn said, as he kicked off his shoes and began to unbutton his pants.

"I'll be right back." I ran down the stairs to find the soap I had bought at that cute little store. I saw the lavender bar and went upstairs again. He had already gotten into the tub, his muscular, sweat-streaked arms sprawled across the rim, and his head tilted back, showing his neck and Adam's apple. He rolled his head to look at me. I was standing there biting my lip, taking him in. God, he looked good dirty.

"This was a good idea," he said with an almost drunk look on his face.

The bathtub wasn't big enough for two people, so I sat on the rim and began to rub his body with the new bar of soap. I started with his shoulders and worked down his arms one at a time. Then, I washed his neck and chest, letting the soap slip down his abs below the water to his thigh.

"I think you missed a spot," he said, as I brought the soap back up out of the water along his leg.

"You're right. Lean forward so I can wash your back." I walked around the tub behind him. He leaned forward, and I lathered my hands up. Using my fingernails, I lightly scratched down his back until I reached his butt and grabbed it hard, then I slowly brought my hands back up to his shoulders. Bjorn abruptly stood up. Water dripped off his beautiful naked body as he turned around and faced me. I saw everything on him was standing.

"I think I'm clean enough," he said, "but you are filthy." He stepped out of the tub and began to undress me.

Bjorn picked me up and sat me on the sink counter. Grabbing me by my hair, he pulled my head back and began kissing my neck. His hot wet body rocked against mine as I held on to him; I moaned. He began to quicken his pace, and then with one final hard thrust, he shivered in my arms.

Not again, I thought. I wasn't anywhere near done with him, but he pulled out of me and went to grab a towel for himself. He walked up to me and caressed my face, then kissed me on the cheek.

"My sweet Emma," he whispered in my ear. "We are leaving in a couple of hours. Try to get a little rest," he said, as he left the bathroom.

I looked at the dirty water in the bathtub and pulled the stopper. I refilled the bath with clean water and got in. *At least it was better than the first time*, I thought, as my hands slipped between my thighs. I thought about his naked, wet body and the way it felt pressed against mine, and I finished what Bjorn should have.

Bjorn woke me at dawn. I looked over at the clock by my bed; it was four a.m. "Did you at least make coffee?" I asked, as I rolled out of bed, but I felt awake as soon as I stood up. I was too excited to be sleepy. So, this was it, today we would return the heart to the beast. Today everyone would become mortal again.

I looked at Bjorn as he came back from the kitchen with a cup of coffee for me. Today was going to be the most important day of his many lifetimes. I was so happy for him.

"Thank you, and happy mortality day," I told him, as I blew on my cup of coffee and took a sip. He sat on my bed for a moment and put his hands to his face.

"You're right. I've been thinking about getting here, that I hadn't stopped to think this is it. This is really it," Bjorn looked like a nervous groom on his wedding day.

"Are you getting cold feet?" I asked.

"No. I'm just letting it finally sink in. This is amazing," he got up and hugged me. I nearly spilled my coffee all over him. "This is amazing," he said again and then left to put my bags in the rental car.

Ragnar was already in the passenger seat. He had turned on the radio and looked very happy as he bobbed his head to the music playing. I dumped the rest of my coffee down the sink, took a quick trip to the toilet, then put my shoes on and grabbed my cloak. I paused to take a deep breath of crisp, country air and then I got into the back seat as Bjorn locked up the house.

It looked like several of Bjorn's men were going to be on the same ferry as us. We got out to greet them, and Bjorn opened the trunk and began to rummage through our luggage.

"Emma?" Bjorn said nervously. "Did you pack the ultrasound suitcase?"

I shook my head. I hadn't seen it since last night. "No, I thought Ivar took it with him and Sigurd," I told him. Bjorn took out his phone and began to call, I assumed, one of his brothers.

"He's not picking up. I think I left it at the house, I need to go back and check." Bjorn walked up to two of his men, and I recognized them, the tall skinny one and the slightly fat one from the thing. They were among the first to stand by me for the vote. "Eric, Gorm, can you take Emma and Ragnar in your car?"

Eric, the taller one, said, "We only have room for one."

Gorm pointed through the window of their car. "The back is packed with camping gear," he explained.

"That's alright, take Emma. My father and I will catch the next ferry." Before Eric and Gorm officially agreed to take me, Bjorn was back in the car and pulling a U-turn in the road.

"Emma!" Eric and Gorm said simultaneously with their arms out and gathered me up in a welcoming sandwich of an embrace.

"What a beautiful day," Gorm said, and I looked up at the grey sky as a raindrop fell on my nose.

"How did we get so lucky to have such a beautiful woman to spend it with," Eric said, as he opened the passenger side of the car and pulled the seat forward for me.

Their two-door hatchback was almost completely full of camping gear, but I managed to move around a few things, Eric took a bag with him on his lap, and I put their other backpack on the floor under my feet, so my knees were almost up to my chest, but we made it work.

"This is a lot of camping gear for an overnight trip," I said from the back.

"We're going to drive across Europe this summer, and then in the autumn, we are going to move to Colorado," Gorm told me, as he drove the car onto the ferry. "We've always been farmers, Erik and I, but we've never tried to grow hydroponically." Eric turned to look at me with a big smile on his young, goofy face.

"Pot farmers in Colorado? I can see you two doing that," I told them.

It started to rain as the ferry pulled away from the dock, but I didn't mind being cramped in the car with Eric and Gorm, they were great company. Soon after the ferry reached its destination, we drove across the mainland of Orkney to Harray Loch. We pulled off the main road, and I could see a roadblock ahead of us. Eric rolled down his window to talk to a young man in a bright orange vest.

"Sorry private event, this road is closed for the day."

"Fuck off, Arne. We've got a V.I.P in the back," Eric said, and the man in the vest looked back at me.

"Emma! Where's Bjorn?" Arne asked.

"He'll be on the next ferry," Gorm told him.

"Stay to the right, and you'll find your way," Arne said, as he patted the top of the car, and we drove on.

We drove a few more minutes down the road, and then I could see the moving truck. Someone was setting up a tent, and a few cars were parked along the side of the road. We parked alongside them. It felt so good to get out of the back of their car. I thanked Eric and Gorm for the ride and then took a much-needed walk to the loch to stretch my legs. I could see Stacey; he was sitting with the body of the beast along the shoreline. He had shaved his head and was wearing a white skirt with slits up both sides but nothing else. He was painting symbols on his exposed chest and arms, and I could see his legs were already covered in the same marks he had painted on my nails.

I walked up to the beast to look at her in the light. She had eight claws on her fan-like feet, each the size of my hand. When I looked at her head, I took a step back and gasped. "When did she open her eyes?"

Stacey looked up at me. "Early this morning. Shortly after, we sat her down by the water."

¤ Thorn of Betrayal ¤

Stacey stood up and held his hand out for me to take. "Will you do me the honor of making me mortal again?"

I took his hand, "Of course, but Bjorn forgot the ultrasound machine; he'll be on the next ferry."

Stacey shook his head and led me up the bank toward the moving truck. "Sigurd and Ivar have it. Everything is set up for you in there," he pointed at the truck.

Ivar saw us walking and ran to greet me. "Emma! Where's Bjorn and Ragnar?" I explained he would be on the next ferry and that Bjorn tried to call. Ivar looked confused, then he pulled out his phone and looked at it. "I don't have a missed call," he said, as he walked away with the phone to his ear.

The truck had a chair and a cot set up inside it and a fold-up table with a clear plastic tub sitting on top of the table for the heart pieces to go in, I assumed. Stacey laid down on the cot, and I turned on the portable ultrasound machine. I gently pressed on Stacey's stomach.

"Are you ready?" I asked. It looked like emotions were about to overflow from him. He didn't speak, but he nodded, so I took the wand and rolled it over his stomach. "There it is. Okay, now let's get it out." I took the tube, and Stacey laid on his side to swallow it. I retrieved the piece of the beast's heart he had swallowed over twelve hundred years ago and placed it in the palm of his hand. Stacey marveled at it for a few moments, then he put it in the tub and thanked me. When I looked out of the truck's open back, I noticed we had an audience. Erik, Gorm, Sigurd, Arne, and a couple of others I hadn't been formally introduced to yet were staring with wide anxious eyes at us. They helped Stacey from the truck and began embracing him. Stacey broke down in joyful tears as he smiled and blessed them all.

One by one, the Vikings took their turn to have the beast's heart removed from them. Sigurd had the two pieces, both showed up on the ultrasound. They hadn't fused together like I worried that they might, but he was the only one with multiple pieces in his stomach so far. He added his pieces to the others in the tub. I looked outside, and the audience had grown. I did the math in my head. If I took about ten minutes for each man, it would take me eight hours to complete all the procedures if I didn't take any breaks.

"Sigurd, can you stay and watch the next few? I'd like you to take over for me when I need a break." I talked out loud and in detail for my next patient, then I let Sigurd try. "Make sure to check for multiple pieces," I told him. He rolled the ultrasound wand over the stomach of the next Viking.

"Take a deep breath," Sigurd told him.

It ended up taking us nearly ten hours, but we managed to remove all the beast's heart from everyone successfully. Except for Ragnar and Bjorn, they still hadn't come by the truck yet. The plastic tub was nearly full of fleshy pieces. I took the tub and gave it a little shake. As soon as a pair of matching pieces touched, they would fuse together.

I jumped down from the truck and stretched. Most of the clouds had cleared, and the ones that remained were pink with the summer's late evening light. I saw Ragnar marching up to the big tent the men had set up earlier in the day and decided to follow him. If he was here, then Bjorn must be too. I wanted to tell them it was their turn. Just as I reached the flap of the tent, I heard Ivar shouting.

"What about Emma!"

I stopped and listened. *What about me?* I felt childish listening outside of the tent, I didn't feel like I was meant to hear this, which made me only want to hear it more.

"You said you'd grow old with her." Was Ivar shouting at Bjorn, I wondered?

"She's too dangerous, Ivar." Was that Bjorn? He sounded different. "That's why I gave the signal for Svetlana to kill the crew of the *Bryony*. I deleted the nautical history of the ship, but she was there. She could tell someone where she dropped the heart."

It felt like someone had just smashed a hammer into my chest. "If Emma's too dangerous, then so am I, so are you!" Ivar shouted back.

"That's a fair point," Ragnar interrupted.

"No, it isn't, you're family. You can be trusted. She's a liability, Ivar."

"Fuck you, Bjorn! You're not killing Emma!" Ivar ran out of the tent and straight into me. One look at my face, and he knew I had heard everything. Ivar grabbed my arm and began running with me away from the tent, but we hadn't gotten very far before I felt someone grab my other arm and pull me away from Ivar.

I looked to see who it was, but I didn't recognize him. "She's not yours!" The young man shouted at Ivar. "She's mine!" And that's when I recognized him. He hadn't gone back for the ultrasound machine; he went back to finish his rejuvenation.

"Bjorn," I said in a small voice. Ivar swung at his brother and hit him square in the nose. Bjorn let go of me, and the brothers began to exchange blows. Bjorn had the advantage; he was still invulnerable, and soon Ivar was a bloody mess, but he kept on fighting until Sigurd and Ragnar pulled him away. All the men came to watch the spectacle.

"Emma is mine now! You can't have her; I won't let you kill her!" Ivar spat blood at his brother. There was a murmur from the other Vikings as they listened to the events unfolding.

Ragnar spoke next, "She's Bjorn's property, Ivar. Unless he

freely gives her to you, you can't lay a claim on her." Bjorn went to grab my arm again.

"No," I told him, but he grabbed it anyway.

I had been looking at the crowd of men around me, looking for a way out, when I saw Stacey. Our eyes locked, and it was as if time froze. My fingertips began to tingle, I looked down at them, and the symbols Stacey had painted glowed a brilliant red. It made me remember something Stacey had said. I looked up, and time had caught up again. I could feel Bjorn begin to pull me away. I let my arm go limp but kept my stance strong.

In a calm and loud voice, so all the men would hear, I said, "I am not your thrall anymore, Bjorn. I am your wife, I am family. And you, you are the *king*. Which makes me, the *queen*!"

Bjorn squeezed my arm painfully, but I refused to flinch. "That was just pretending," Bjorn growled through gritted teeth.

"I witnessed you introduce her as your wife," Ragnar said.

"And I witnessed you consummate your marriage," Ivar added as a victorious, bloody grin spread across his face.

"She's family," Ragnar declared, "and you've elevated her status to royalty. She has caused no infraction that warrants death—"

"If you wish to divorce her," Ivar interrupted his father, "then I'll marry her, brother."

Bjorn let go of my arm. I couldn't tell what he was thinking, his face was like a statue. Then, he looked at me and said, "We'll celebrate our marriage later." He began to walk toward the moving truck. "Sigurd, I'll need a hand!"

Sigurd let go of Ivar and followed him. Ragnar did the same. Ivar rushed to me and picked me up off the ground as he spun me around in his embrace. "You are a clever, clever fox!" he said and put me down. "And officially my sister!" he told me, and I began to cry hysterically.

"They are all dead? The whole crew? Captain Youssef and Richie? All because I dropped the heart in the ocean?"

Ivar held on to me so I wouldn't fall to the ground. "It's not your fault, Emma. That kind of power is just too tempting. The water there is shallow. The captain saw an immortal man pulled from the ocean. Kings have sent leagues of men to their deaths to look for the Holy Grail, and this is no different. They would search for it for generations. Whole countries would go to war over that water space just for the *chance* that they might find the ultimate weapon. A chance at immortality. No one can know where it is."

Bjorn had said he knew the captain's family for generations, and I'd thought he trusted him. He had known me for what, a month?

"What's Bjorn going to do with me?"

Ivar looked down at his feet. "He won't kill you, and he won't divorce you. That means he intends to keep you."

A chill ran down my body. Maybe I should've chosen death. Just as I finished the thought, I heard the low melancholy tone of the horn being blown. I turned toward the sound and saw Sigurd with the horn. Bjorn was standing beside him, holding the beast's completed, beating heart above his head with both hands.

Ivar linked our arms together at the elbow, and we walked toward the beach, the men had started a fire and were gathering around it. The sun was beginning to set, and the water of the loch was red as blood. Everyone took a knee except for the high priest. He stood naked, a dagger hanging around his neck. His skin was covered in white symbols, and with his hands held out in front of him, he walked over to his kneeling king and took the beast's heart from Bjorn's hands.

Stacey's body began to sway, his hands holding the heart turned toward my direction and seemed to be pulling him directly to me. "Stacey?" I asked, as I looked up into his face, but he didn't answer. His eyes were rolled in the back of his head, and he was holding the heart out to me.

"Stand up, Emma," Ivar whispered to me. I stood, and as I did, the heart swung Stacey around, and he started walking toward the shore. Stacey paused and looked back at me. "Follow him," Ivar whispered. I took a step toward Stacey, and he looked ahead again. I took another step, and so did he. He only stepped when I stepped; it was as if I was leading Stacey to the beach, even though I was behind him.

Stacey reached the body of the beast first, and I went to stand by his side. He lowered her heart into the center of her splintered body. Then, Stacey took the dagger from around his neck and cut his hand, but his cut healed immediately. "It's okay, take mine," I offered him my hand, and without a word, he sliced deeply into my palm. I hissed at the sharp shock but stood still and held my bleeding hand over her heart. I could feel my heartbeat in the cut, and the beast's heartbeat began to beat in sync with my own.

With every beat, the splinters began to move, like they were made of sand and poured in around her heart. Soon her gaping wound looked whole again, and after a few more moments, her scales began to stand up along her spine. I wanted to back away, but Stacey stood behind me and had a firm grip on my shoulders. She picked up her head and turned it toward me. A hiss escaped her opening mouth as her long spiked black tongue darted in and out.

"I'm not your enemy," I told her. Suddenly, she stood and faced me. She shook her powerful body. And then reached up with her giant front fan-like paw and held one of her black, sharp claws an inch away from my eye. I stood frozen with fear.

"I have seen," Stacey said in a strange hiss-like voice that was not his own. The beast moved her claw to my ear. "I have listened," Stacey continued. Then, she moved her claw to my chest. "I have felt everything!" The beast slowly took her claw and cut an X into my chest over my heart.

Her claw burned like fire and radiated through my body. But I couldn't move; the pain reminded me of when I was drowning in the ocean. My lungs felt like they were burning; I thought I was dying, but then I remembered the piece of the beast's heart in my hand. I had a choice; until this very moment, I didn't even remember making it. But I had chosen life. I had swallowed the piece of immortal heart I held, clutched in my fist with a mouth of saltwater. In my moment of need, it felt like it was...

"A gift," Stacey said, as the beast backed away from me and began to walk toward the water.

Stacey let go of my shoulders and followed her. She stopped and bent her front knees at the shoreline to let Stacey climb onto her back. Then, she stood again and slowly walked into the water. Her scales began to reflect the last of the day's light, and she became almost translucent as if she was made of water herself. She dove into the loch, taking Stacey with her.

"Stacey!" I called, but the water was still. There wasn't even a ripple where she had dove under the surface.

¤ *A New Island* ¤

Most of the men said their goodbyes and left shortly after Stacey and the water horse disappeared, including Bjorn. I think some of the men were afraid to spend the night by the water in case she came back to get revenge on them.

Ivar waited by the shore with me as I scanned the water with a flashlight. I don't think he thought Stacey would come back, but he stayed and searched anyway. When the batteries in his flashlight finally died, he turned to me with a sad smile and a nod.

"Goodbye," I said to the dark water of the loch and walked back to the fire, which was only glowing embers and ashes. "What happens now?" I asked Ivar, as I stood and tried to warm myself on the last of the fire's heat.

"You'll come home with me," Ivar said. "Until Bjorn comes back for you. Tonight, we camp under the stars." Ivar took a log of firewood and fed the hungry embers. I looked up, but I couldn't see very many stars. It was getting cloudy again, and I wondered if it might rain. Ivar looked up as well and took a deep breath through his nose. "We still have the moving truck if it starts to rain," he said, as if he was reading my mind.

As the fire began to come alive again, Sigurd joined us. He brought me my cloak and the first aid kit. "Let's have a look at your hand," Sigurd said. I put my cloak around my shoulders, and we sat down together by the fire. "It looks clean. You might need stitches, but that will have to wait until the morning." Sigurd squeezed out a little packet of antibacterial ointment and wrapped my hand with a sterile gauze bandage. "Do you want me to look at the wound on your chest?" he asked me.

"Yes, my hand doesn't hurt so much, but my chest burns." I pulled my cloak down off my shoulders. My shirt was red with blood from where the beast had used her claws to carve an X into me.

"Turn a little more toward the light for me, Emma," Sigurd said. He took an alcohol whip and dapped at the wound. "It's a little swollen," he said, as he squeezed out another little pack of antibacterial ointment onto the mark. He taped on a bandage and then dug around in his first aid kit. "These are the neatest things," he twisted a little bag and shook it. "Instant ice packs. Did you know they make heat ones too?" he asked, as he handed me the icepack. "I've been thinking about getting back into medicine," he said with a smile on his face.

"You did great today," I told him and pressed the ice pack over my bandage.

"What happened down at the shore? Why did the beast mark you like that?" Ivar asked me with a concerned tone to his voice.

"I thought she was going to eat me," I said in all honesty. "The beast, she used Stacey, the high priest, to tell me she had heard, and seen, and felt everything through all of you." Ivar and Sigurd looked at each other with wide eyes. "I think she wanted me to give you something. A message."

Ivar and Sigurd leaned in closer to me. "What was it?" Sigurd asked. I paused for a moment and looked at them.

"Fuck you!" I yelled at them, as I flipped them my middle finger. Ivar and Sigurd stared at me for a second and then burst out laughing. "Good night," I told them both and gave Ivar a kiss on the cheek. I wrapped my cloak around myself again and walked to the moving truck.

I was glad I claimed the cot in the back of the truck early. Sometime in the middle of the night, I woke up to the sound of the truck's doors slamming and rain pinging off the top of its metal roof. I woke up at dawn and sat up in my cot and unwrapped the bandage on my hand. The cut had completely healed. I pressed on my palm and flexed my fingers; there wasn't even a red line left. It was as though it never even happened.

"Shit," I said, as I remembered Sigurd was going to want to look at it again in the light. I took off the pin holding my cloak together and hissed through my teeth as I cut a new wound, then I rewrapped my hand in the old bandage.

"I don't think you'll need stitches," Sigurd said as he examined my hand.

"That's a relief," I told him.

"How's your chest?" he asked.

Oddly enough, it hadn't healed like my hand. "It's okay, it stings, though," I told Sigurd, as I pulled the neck of my shirt down to let him change the wound dressing.

"If you feel like you are getting a fever, or if you see red lines begin to run from it, let me know, and I'll get you antibiotics," Sigurd said, and he handed me another instant ice pack.

"Let's go, or we'll miss the first ferry," Ivar said and opened the passenger side door of the truck for me.

"You know, you can just let me go," I told Ivar during the ferry ride.

"That's not a good idea, Emma," Sigurd said. "Bjorn isn't that mad, but if you run now… Trust me; it could be a lot worse."

I thought about that for a moment, "I can fake my own death."

Ivar laughed and said, "You think someone who's been faking his death for over a thousand years would fall for that?"

Sigurd leaned forward so he could see me better. "The anticipation of what he might do to you is worse than what he will do."

I took a deep breath. *Okay*, I thought, *I'm just overthinking it*. Besides, I probably wasn't going to see Bjorn for a couple of days. I looked forward to spending time at Ivar's house. It had such a comfortable and slightly retro feel to it. However, my hopes were quickly smashed as I saw a familiar rental car come into view as we drove around the bend and arrived at Ivar's house.

A very young Bjorn was sitting at the kitchen table with a folder of papers in front of him. When he saw me, he didn't get up, but he did smile. "Sit down, Emma. I got you a wedding present." Bjorn placed the folder across from him on the table. I picked it up and opened it. There were several printed-off pages of pictures of an island from different angles.

"What's this?" I asked him; it wasn't what I'd expected.

"Turn to the second page." I flipped the first page of the pictures over. There was a little house on the island, and these were the interior pictures. It looked kind of nice, like maybe it was a vacation home or used for weekend fishing trips. I flipped to the next page. It was the listing price, and it had a big red sold stamped across it. "I bought you an island, Emma. Do you like it?"

Bjorn bought me a small five-kilometer island off the coast of Orkney as a wedding present. It had a small cottage that seemed airy and loved. It looked like there was once a raised garden on one of its sides. In truth and on paper, I did like it very much. However, the only way to get on the island was by boat, and as I stood on the island, looking out over the sea, and watched Bjorn sail away in that boat, I wasn't sure I liked it after all.

"I've arranged for a boat to pick up your trash every other Wednesday," Bjorn had said before he left. "You can leave your shopping list with it on the dock. I've told the boatman you have leprosy, and you are highly contagious, so to never come in direct contact with you. I'll visit you once a year, my dear wife."

"Fuck you, Bjorn, you're a cruel bastard," I said, as I watched his boat grow smaller in the distance. *You could have at least given me WIFI.*

The cottage had one bedroom and was sparsely furnished. It had a strange musky smell, and I spent the rest of the day cleaning with the windows open. Electricity came from a solar panel and a little wind turbine on the roof. A large rainwater barrel that sat on stilts provided the cottage with water. There was a wa-

morning. Sigurd and the boat were gone, and thankfully, so was the mouse-infested mattress. I watered my new houseplant and played music from my laptop, and I realized I was smiling. It was still a prison, but it was beginning to feel like home too. My cell phone binged; it was a text message from Ivar.

It's the second day at school, and I'm enjoying the curriculum, especially history. I just can't stand all these damn children, he wrote with a winking face and included a selfie in front of the school smiling.

Sigurd came back to the island just after sunset. This time I thought to put a bandage on the palm of my hand. Yesterday, he didn't seem to notice my hand was perfectly fine; at least, I hoped he hadn't. I walked down to the dock to meet him, and he handed me a box with holes in the side. I heard loud little meows coming from the box and opened it immediately.

"Oh my, look at you two," I told the two little furballs that began to climb out of the box and onto me. One was grey with white paws, and the other was white with grey paws.

"The farmer assured me their mother is a fierce mouser. They should grow to be vicious rodent killers," Sigurd said, as he struggled with a box he was pulling from his boat. "This is a memory foam mattress. And it's heavier than it looks. It should inflate to normal size in an hour once you open the box." He carried the boxed-up mattress up to the cottage, and I brought the kittens.

"What should I name you?" I asked my new little fur babies.

¤ *Death in the Family* ¤

A year seemed like such a long time when I counted the days. Sitting here now and looking back at the last twenty, it's true what they say. It all went by in a blink. I smiled when I thought back on some of my favorite moments. Ivar would sneak out to come to visit me. He even pulled an elaborate island prison break every December so I could see the Christmas market. It was easier for Ivar to visit once he looked old enough to be independent. Then, he came to visit almost every day until Rosaline's granddaughter, Lilian, came to stay with her for a summer. Ivar fell in love with Lilian almost as soon as he saw her and followed her to university in Glasgow.

He still sends me text messages and photos, but it's rare for him to visit anymore. Ivar and Lilian have four children together, three girls and one boy, and he did end up with a dadbod, which he is very proud of growing.

Sigurd became a doctor for Doctors without Borders. I hadn't seen him for years. I even made a new social media account to post photos of my garden and cats, and that's how I followed most of Sigurd's adventures. He found his true passion in helping people, and I was happy for him, but I also missed him very much.

The two kittens he brought me all those years ago, Bob and Dylan, did grow up to be excellent mousers. I looked over at my garden, where I had placed two stones over their graves. Dylan, the grey one with white paws, had just passed away this spring, and Bob died in the winter three years ago. I missed their company most of all. Ivar offered to bring me a new cat, but I told him my heart just wasn't ready to replace them yet.

Bjorn moved back to his resort, and he kept his promise, visiting once a year, usually to watch the sunset on the summer solstice. That was why he was here now. We were sitting outside, talking and watching the setting sun on the longest day of the year. He had brought a bottle of Scotch to celebrate with me. I went inside and prepared a pair of crystal whiskey glasses. They reminded me of his crystal champagne glass I had knocked over all those years ago in his office.

The whiskey glasses were a gift from Bjorn for my 50th birthday. It was hard to believe that was already ten years ago. I caught my reflection in the kitchen window. My hair has gone completely grey, and my skin weathered from all the time I spent outside in the garden, but I was still fit. I don't have very many smile lines, and my mouth corners seem to be permanently downturned. I thought I looked like a bitter old woman, and I supposed I was.

Turning around to go back outside, I paused for a moment to think. Had I fed my latest hobby today? I walked over to my bedroom and looked closely at the colorful saltwater aquarium. I had it delivered a couple of months ago with my biweekly shopping request. "Here, fishes. I have stinky flakes for you. Your favorite." I watched as the colorful fish came to the top of the tank to eat their flakes. The pufferfish was my favorite. He swam around with the other fish, and they had no idea how dangerous he was. I would spend hours watching my fish swim in and out of their colorful fake coral reef.

I went back outside and placed the two glasses between us. "So, what's happened since our last visit?" I asked Bjorn, as I sat down and opened the bottle of Scotch he had brought.

"Ragnar died. He had a heart attack," Bjorn told me.

"Congratulations," I offered. Normally, it would be condolences, but it was really something to celebrate for someone who made it to his age.

Bjorn laughed and nodded as he took the Scotch bottle from me and poured us both a glass. "It's something worth celebrating, you're right," he handed me one of the glasses. "Wait, let's take a photo." He pulled out his phone. We leaned our bodies closer together, he still smelled like peppermint aftershave, and he took a photo.

"Here's to Ragnar, the legend," I said, and we toasted our glasses together. Bjorn drank his Scotch in one big gulp and made a satisfied grunting noise. He took a deep breath and looked out over the water.

"It's funny, I'm about to turn forty for the last time, but I feel like life is just beginning." Bjorn's face looked content and was glowing with the light of the sunset. I enjoyed a quiet moment with him and listened for a sizzle as the sun hit the water. I thought about the fireworks from twenty years ago, how they popped and sizzled as they fell in streamers into the ocean and how I had missed the last toast to a perfect day.

"Did I ever tell you about my friend Rachel? She was nineteen, I couldn't imagine being that young again, but I'm looking forward to fully enjoying my forties." I looked over at Bjorn, but he wasn't listening. Instead, he was staring at the sunset.

"I can see Valhalla," he said with wonderous big bright eyes and a slightly slack jaw. He was barely holding on to his empty Scotch glass. Bjorn swayed ever so gently in his chair like he was dancing in a beautiful dream. But all dreams end, even for thousand-year-old Vikings. As Bjorn let out his last breath, the sky turned a brilliant bright red, and his lips were now a pale shade of blue. I watched a small trickle of foam from his mouth begin to run down his clean-shaven chin.

I leaned over Bjorn and kissed him on his forehead. Then, I took Bjorn's phone out of his hand. "Will you look at that? It's not even locked. You really should be more careful. Someone could access your whole life from here." I held the Scotch up to my nose and inhaled its rich oaky scent as I scrolled through Bjorn's emails. Bjorn was dead, which meant I was finally free. "Here's to the first of many new beginnings," I toasted to myself.

The End

ACKNOWLEDGEMENTS

To my cheerleaders and beta readers, Liz, Tisha, Lynn, Ariel, and Joy. Your kind words and enthusiasm gave me the confidence to continue writing.

Thank you, Kate, for being the voice of Emma. Mary for repeatedly jumping into my neighbor's pool so I could film footage for the book trailer. And thank you to my neighbor Herb for letting us use his pool.

LA Morris designed the cover, Kelly Carter designed and formatted the interior, Whitney's Book Works did the line and copy editing, and Nele Diel created custom art. Ladies, you truly deserve a round of applause. Thank you so much for making *The Immortal* look good.

Other faces that need a kiss on the cheek and a big thank you are Mason, Merritt, Jake, and Jonathan.

Last but not least, to my beautiful baby boys, you were the biggest pain in my backend while I was trying to write this book, but I love you with all my heart, and I don't think I would have done it without you.

Printed in Great Britain
by Amazon